STEVIE

"What in the hell do you think you're doing?" I looked up from the computer, where my focus had been trained for the past two hours, and my gaze slammed right into a pair of angry green eyes. Angry, but beautiful eyes that weren't quite mossy green and not quite forest, but somewhere in between. And definitely angry. "Well? I asked you a question."

He hadn't really asked so much as *barked* the words at me but saying so now would only poke the bear. No, not a bear. A beast. The man I guessed was my new boss was a big beast of a man, with shoulders so wide he had to turn just to get into the office and a broad chest that even his pricey Oxford couldn't contain. His narrow waist suggested that at some point in time he'd been an athlete —that, and the way he carried himself, graceful and sure. He had ashy blond hair that would probably curl if he ever let it grow long enough, and those green eyes, well, it made him one hell of a package. A big, sexy, and very angry package.

"I won't ask again."

Right. He wanted to know what I was doing here.

"I'm updating the filing system. This one, if it can even be called a filing system, is out of date. Way, way out of date. My guess is you have plenty of money you haven't been paid yet." How could a man with his pedigree, if his business partner was to be believed, run his business this way? "Do you need something?"

I was his assistant, after all. It was part of the job, as it always was. I didn't love it, but I could handle it.

The beast's nostrils flared. "I need for you to tell me why you're on *my* computer doing *anything at all* to *my* filing system." I opened my mouth to tell him exactly who I was, but he held up two big paws—I mean, hands—and glared. "Step away from the computer."

This whole routine was already getting tired, but I needed this job, so I stood, slowly, summoning every dollop of patience I had, and stepped away from the computer. With my hands up. This *was* Texas, after all, plus it was guaranteed to piss him off. "I'm your new vet assistant. Your business partner, Eddy, hired me."

The older woman was a little bit kooky, but she was nice and blunt, which made her my kind of people.

"Eddy hired—" His words cut off abruptly and he shook his head as a few more choice expletives spilled from his mouth. "Eddy is in no position to hire anyone. Period."

HERO BOSS

AN ALPHA MALE OFFICE ROMANCE

PIPER SULLIVAN

She had mentioned that he was a stubborn man but now, staring up at him and seeing the genuine anger and confusion on his face, I wondered if I should have waited to talk to him. I'd wanted to, but Eddy insisted he was busy and happy to have her deal with all the details. Dammit, this is what happened when you didn't think first, just acted. It was kind of my specialty and, oddly enough, exactly why I needed this job to start with. "Well, Eddy *did* hire me, and I need this job. Now you're telling me you don't even need an assistant?" Arms folded, I looked at the big man in the deep green shirt with darker green buttons. He looked like the last doctor I'd worked for—the only difference was his patients were animals.

"No, I'm not saying that," he conceded and blew out a long breath.

"But you don't want *me* to be your assistant?" I didn't look exactly like what anyone wanted in an executive assistant, but I more than made up for it by being excellent at my job. Stuffed-shirts didn't mind the nose ring or row of studs that went up my left ear when I made their lives easier than their wives did.

"I didn't say that, either."

"You're not saying much of anything, Dr. Henderson." When he blinked, I lowered my arms, enjoying the small smirk that played across his mouth. "And the state of your filing system says you could use the help, so what is it? The piercings?"

Guys like him always judged a book by its cover when their covers never matched the contents inside.

"I didn't say it was anything!" He smacked his hands on the round edges of the circular reception desk. "You're frustrating, you know that?"

It wasn't the first time I'd heard that, so I nodded. "I'm not the one turning away a damn good assistant because she doesn't fit my own preconceived notions."

His green eyes narrowed to slits and his nostrils flared, harder this time. I had to clench my jaw and school my features into a bored expression. He was intimidating, but he wasn't scary. "Got me all figured out, don't you?"

"No, and I don't *want* to figure you out. I want a job, and this happens to be a job I'm damn good at. I don't get what the problem is because you won't tell me."

After a few long moments of silence, his shoulders dropped in resignation. "There's nothing wrong with my filing system."

That's what he wanted to focus on? Okay. "So, you have twenty-seven different horses with a hoof infection to check out today?" His face paled at the information and I knew I'd proven my point, even if I'd had to exaggerate it a little bit. "I didn't think so. Do you have any idea who's current on their bills and who's delinquent?"

"No."

"I already have a list running. Or should I toss it out because this business is the one special business that doesn't need to turn a profit?" My specialty was small businesses just like this. Give me a few months and I'd have this place running like a well-oiled machine.

"Who are you?" The question, this time, was asked

with a little less venom than before so I smiled and held one hand out.

"Stevie Mattis. Organizer and assistant extraordinaire. Eddy said you needed help and it's a pay bump from my last job, so I accepted." And I kept my hand there, dangling alone in the air until he did what every proper southern boy was raised to do: be respectful.

His big hand swallowed mine up. It was hot and oddly smooth. Too hot. I snatched my hand back to avoid being burned and waited for him to say something. Anything. "One week. We'll do a one-week trial run to see how well we work together. If it doesn't work out, you won't try to get my grandma to change my mind."

I frowned. "Dude, I don't even know your grandma."

His eyebrows arched high. "Eddy is my grandmother. Not my business partner."

After a beat of silence, a loud laugh erupted out of me. I shook my head at the sheer *Hallmark*-ness of it all. "A meddling grandmother, huh? I never would've guessed. She doesn't sound all that grandmotherly."

"Well, that's Eddy. Do we have a deal?"

Damn straight, we did. "Yep." I was good at my job and I knew by the middle of the week he'd be asking me to stay, so I wasn't worried. "Eddy said you take your coffee with two creams and two sugars, is that right?" He nodded and I turned towards the small break room in the back. "I'll grab you a cup while you get settled. Then we can talk about whatever is on your mind."

He stared at me like he couldn't quite figure me out,

nodding slowly as if distracted, before he turned and disappeared around the corner into his office.

I hurried to make sure the coffee was hot, grabbing a pastry because sugar and carbs made everyone a little easier to deal with—especially busy doctors prone to crankiness.

*C*losing the office door behind me so I could fume in peace, I took several deep breaths after that frustrating encounter with that... that *frustrating* woman. Stevie, what the hell kind of name was that for a woman, anyway? Especially a professional woman—even though she hardly looked professional, in jeans that hugged her ass and thighs like a lover and a ring in her nose. No, Eddy had gone too far with her meddling this time. Interfering in my love life was one thing, but my business was where I drew the line.

I hung up the blazer I brought because it was ingrained into me to dress professionally, even though my patients all had four legs and didn't give a damn what I wore. Dropping my beat-up brown leather bag on the floor beside my desk, I lowered myself into the chair and let out a sigh. It was too early for a headache, but already, I felt one coming on. So much for showing up early to get a jump start on the day.

But on top of my desk was Stevie's resume. No, not Stevie—Stephanie. Stephanie Ann Mattis from Gary, Indiana. She was a long way from home, but she had an impressive work history that made me wonder why she'd taken this job in the middle of nowhere.

"Why?" It was the only question I had. If Stevie looked a little different, I might have thought it was Eddy's attempt at matchmaking, but she wasn't my type at all. She was too short, too curvy, and had way too much sass. If it wasn't about romance, then Eddy must be worried about me—and that was the last thing I wanted. An assistant was the last thing I wanted.

A knock sounded on the door a second before it opened and Stevie strode in, her strides quick and capable. "Here's your coffee." She offered the oversized mug with a smile and earned extra points for not making a joke about the 'Stay Pawsitive' printed on the front of the mug. I watched as she rounded the desk and took the chair across from me. "Did you want to start with the filing system?"

She wasn't in charge here. I was. "I had an assistant once, Stephanie."

"The name is Stevie," she corrected. It was the only thing she said but her gaze remained steady on mine, waiting for me to continue.

"Her name was Tori and I relied on her, as one grows to do, and she did a damn good job. One day, she came in to tell me her boyfriend had proposed and they were moving to Canada together so he could have a real shot at the rodeo. In Canada, when they were already in Texas."

Even thinking about it pissed me off all over again. "I went through a few temps who ran the gamut of just plain incompetent to husband-hunting. I gave up, and for the past eighteen months, I've been doing it all."

She nodded like she understood and I wondered if this would be easier than I thought. "I get that, I really do. The problem is that you haven't been doing it all that well."

"Excuse me?" Didn't she understand that I was the one in the position of authority here?

Stevie stood and set down her notebook so she was free to pace in front of my office. I didn't like it, but it gave me time to observe her. She was a tiny little thing, and she looked younger than the twenty-six her resume suggested she was. Maybe it was her massive black ponytail or the almost indecent white t-shirt she wore that molded over a pair of breasts too large for her petite frame. She didn't wear a lot of makeup, which contributed to her youthful appearance, with smooth white skin marred only by one freckle beneath her right eye. The way she paced, the way her leg muscles bunched with every move, said Stevie wasn't one to sit still. She probably spent a great deal of time outdoors.

Like me.

"Look, I get that you don't like the way this went down and, honestly, I don't either. I packed up my life and moved here because I had a job, so why don't you tell me what I can do to help you accept this?" She finally stopped pacing and stopped right in front of my desk, violet eyes, eerie and bold, staring at me with barely restrained patience.

Instead of answering, I reached for the mug and took a long, fortifying sip. I didn't want her as my assistant but I had no good reason to explain it, so I'd give her the week to show her true self before firing her. "Tuesdays and Thursdays I reserve for field work, going to the farms and ranches in the area. Even if I don't have a standing appointment, preventative care is a priority."

She nodded and scooped up her notebook, scribbling notes on the first page before those clear violet eyes turned back to me. "Do you have special equipment or tools you regularly take for those visits?"

I blinked. "Uh, it varies from week to week." It was a good question. Unexpected, just like Stevie.

She jotted that down, keeping her gaze fixed on mine. "Next?"

I nodded and continued. "Some of the older patients with pets come in and I know they're on a fixed menu so I take the treats they offer. Cooked goods only. No live animals and no huge sides of raw meat. Not anymore."

Stevie's face blossomed into a grin, which quickly transformed into a laugh. It wasn't rusty, it was husky and well used, like she laughed a lot. "Learned that the hard way, huh?"

"Unfortunately." My lips twitched but I controlled myself because it was best to start as you meant to go on —at least, according to Eddy. "I try not to turn anyone away who has an animal in need, but I always like to know beforehand if treatment will be costly."

"So you can decide before you do anything expensive?"

There wasn't any judgment in her eyes or her voice,

but the question still rubbed me the wrong way. "No. There are grants and other services available that I can use if I know ahead of time."

"Cool," she said and scribbled more notes and then a few more, before turning earnest eyes back up to me. Stevie asked a few questions about insurance and new patient information but otherwise, she was quiet. Reserved, even.

"Any other questions?"

"Nope." She shook her head, the mass of thick black curls nearly blinding her. "I'll write them all done so you can answer them all at once. It'll be a better use of our time that way." She stood and held the notepad close, like a barrier between us. "Anything else, Dr. Henderson?"

"No, Stephanie. That will be all."

Her gaze narrowed and her jaw clenched. "My name is Stevie. I only answer to Stevie."

So, she did get riled up. Good to know. I gave a short nod and she turned on her heels and walked to the door. "Good luck, Stephanie."

She stopped in the doorway and turned to me, slowly, with a mischievous smile on her face. "Thanks, Scotty. Lookin' forward to it." Her smile darkened deviously and then she shut the door, giving her the last word.

This time.

Only time would tell if Stevie was as capable as she seemed to think. If she was and had no interest in becoming the Mrs. to my Dr., then she might last more than a week. The other woman, however, would require a firmer approach and when I heard the smile in her voice on the other end of the line, I knew it would be impossible to stay mad at her. But I had to try. "What in the *actual* hell, Grandma?"

Any other grandmother would admonish me for my language, but not Eddy—she cackled for several long minutes before she got herself under control. "Is that any way to speak to your dear old grandmother?"

She was dear to me, but Eddy wasn't anyone's idea of a typical grandmother. She didn't dress the part and certainly didn't act it—she barely acted her age half the time. "It is when she starts to meddle in my business." I shook my head at my own arrogance, thinking that just because the meddling old women in town hadn't focused on me yet, that they'd forgotten about me. "Why, Grandma?"

"I still own that land, I'll remind you." She did, but only because she refused to admit she wasn't as young and quick as she used to be. Her laughter sounded at my silence, and I was glad she couldn't see the smile forming on my face. "I did it because you're working yourself too hard trying to do it all on your own. Your grandfather tried that, too, and got a heart attack for his efforts. What's the problem, you don't like Stevie?"

She really didn't get it. Eddy was bossy as hell and she came from a different time, where her meddling was seen as her due. "I prefer to hire my own employees, Eddy."

"But you don't even have the time to place an ad, never mind to interview applicants. I did it all for you."

I didn't miss the hint of hurt in her voice, and I kicked myself.

"I know you're just trying to help, but I don't know anything about this woman. You gave her a key to my offices! What if she's some kind of criminal?" People came in all the time in search of drugs, and several vet friends of mine had been robbed by tweakers in search of a good high.

A throat cleared behind me and I turned my chair away from the best view in all of Tulip and back to the blank eyes of my new—and temporary—assistant. "The sheriff called. There's a cow giving birth on Old Frontage Road."

I waited for her to say more, to glare at me, but she turned away without another word. I wasn't foolish enough to think that was the end of it, but I was hopeful. "I gotta go, Grandma, there's an emergency. And please, no more meddling."

She laughed but she didn't agree, so I stayed on the line as I gathered what I needed for my bag. "Just give Stevie a chance. She has excellent references and you could use her help."

"Fine. I'll talk to you later." There wouldn't be any harm in letting someone help me out this week, but I made no promises beyond that.

"Tomorrow for dinner. I'll see you then, Scotty." She ended the call on another laugh and I shook my head. Eddy was the most maddening woman alive. She meddled like nobody's business, but she did it out of the goodness of her heart, which made it difficult to stay mad at her—which, of course, meant she never learned her lesson.

She cooked better than anyone in Tulip, though, and

I'd happily show up for dinner and deal with inappropriate conversation and endless amounts of meddling. Her barbecue brisket was worth it. And so was her mac & cheese. Thinking of tomorrow's feast, I strode out of my office and stopped in front of Stevie, whose brows were furrowed as she stared at the computer screen. "Reschedule my appointments if I'm not back in an hour."

"Will do!" The excitement in her voice sounded genuine, but the fact that she refused to look up at me spoke volumes. Luckily, I didn't have time to deal with it now. It was just another item postponed until later, that elusive time in the future that never quite arrived.

STEVIE

*I*t had been a long time since I'd lived in a small town, but getting up early reminded me of what I missed about it. The quiet of the dawn, when everyone who was awake wore a smile even though they were up before the sun. They all tossed out friendly waves and smiles, even to a complete stranger. I could stroll from my motel to the only public parking lot in the city in minutes and even the drive to the Henderson Vet Clinic on the other side of Tulip was quick.

I got up early enough to take a shower and grab some breakfast from the diner, arriving at the office to give myself at least ninety minutes of alone time to catch up on filing. Dr. Henderson filled up a room, either because of his size or the tension he regularly carried around with him. Whatever the reason, it was better for me to get in early and get the day started, if for no other reason than to prove to him that I wasn't a criminal.

Jackass.

That was all right, because I wasn't offended. Not at all. In fact, it was refreshing to know that there was nothing I could do to impress him. Either Dr. Henderson would appreciate my work ethic or he wouldn't. All I could do was my job. For however long I had it.

"Good morning." His deep voice ripped away the peaceful silence and I snatched in a breath before turning my gaze up to the big man.

"Morning, Doc. Would you like your messages now, or do you want them with your coffee?" He was confused by my behavior but too polite or relieved to say so.

"Uh." He raked a hand through his thick blond hair with a sigh. "We can do it with the coffee. Please." It looked like there was more he wanted to say but he stopped himself, shaking his head before he turned and walked away.

And I absolutely did not take an extra long moment to stare at his ass, even though it *was* a mighty fine ass. It was my boss' ass, I had to keep reminding myself. Just because I was new in town didn't mean I had to turn my boss into the star of my sexual fantasies—there was a whole town full of men I didn't have to see every day for that. I stood and made my way to the break room, since the best way to cure yourself of a crush was to serve a man. He was my boss. My off-limits, doctor boss who liked his coffee with cream and sugar. I fixed it and grabbed his messages on the way back to his office.

"Come in."

I rolled my eyes at his need to keep his office door closed when it was just the two of us. But I reminded myself that distance was a good thing. If I'd maintained a bit more, I might have kept my last job. *Yeah, right.* Nothing would have changed the outcome, I knew that. Still, I'd started to like San Antonio. *Oh, well,* I thought bitterly and pushed inside the office. I was rewarded for my efforts by the scowl on his face, which I barely saw thanks to the fine display of corded muscles and blond hair dusting his forearms. "No cancellations so far on today's runs," I told him and handed off the messages before taking a step back.

Distance.

Dr. Henderson stared at me for a long minute, and I was half-tempted to run my tongue across my teeth just in case there was a piece of bacon stuck in there. Then I remembered that he thought I was a criminal. And I remembered what I was wearing. It wasn't an outfit that screamed outlaw, but based on the way he stared at me, a gray t-shirt and black jeans was indeed a criminal uniform. "About what I said yesterday."

My shoulders sank in defeat. I'd hoped to get out of having this conversation at all but I had higher hopes of hanging on to this job, so I nodded but I made sure to let my disinterest show. "What about it?"

I saw the precise moment the hope was extinguished from his green eyes. He'd been hoping I would make this easy on him, but I wasn't that kind of girl. "I didn't mean anything by it. I mean, nothing personal, you know?"

"So, you thinking that I'm a criminal wasn't a personal slight on my character. Got it." I did say I wasn't that kind of girl, right?

"Stevie." The way he said my name, like he already knew me and was exasperated by me, didn't bode well for my chances of continued employment.

"Don't worry about it, Dr. Henderson. You don't know me and I don't expect you to trust me." Not yet, anyway. But like all the doctors before him, he'd see that I wasn't what he thought.

"I don't think you're a criminal." He almost barked the words at me, which made it hard to believe, but I didn't say that to him. "I was trying to make a point to Eddy."

Eddy. Again. Family dynamics had gotten in the way of my last job, costing me a good job in a town I was just starting to like. I wasn't in the mood to start liking a place where I wouldn't be sticking around for long. "Just tell me now if I should be looking for another job, Doc." I didn't care about any of this crap with him and his grandmother, only my ability to pay my rent from one month to the next.

"We said one week."

"Yeah, we did. But you've already made up your mind, I just can't tell which way you're leaning."

Surprise flashed on his face, but quickly on its heels came indecision and it didn't take a genius to figure out what he was thinking about. If he was honest, he was worried I wouldn't stay the rest of the week, because the stubborn man refused to admit that already I'd made his life easier. But he wanted to just leave me hanging to guarantee I stuck around for the next few days. Like my grandpa used to tell me, being a good person is hard. And Dr. Henderson wanted to be a good person.

He nodded, acknowledging that he had made up his mind. "You seem capable enough. So far."

Ah, the negotiation.

I folded my arms and stared right back at him. "I'm not taking a pay cut."

His lips twitched and, once again, he pushed the smile back down. "I'm not asking you to."

Okay. "Then what are you asking? Because I'm not spreading my legs to keep this job."

He frowned. "Where have you worked?"

I arched a brow at him. "Seriously? It's called the world, you should visit it sometime."

The expression of anger mixed with disdain was a good look on him, it hardened his soft appearance. "I'm doing ranch runs today, which means *we're* doing ranch runs today."

I tried not to be offended at the hope and glee that transformed him from good looking to gorgeous at the thought that getting up close with the animals would send me running. I was used to people like him not wanting me around. It was too damn bad for Dr. Henderson that I wanted this job. Needed it, really. "Sounds good. What time do we leave?"

"You have the schedule, Stevie."

Smart ass. "I do, but you know something I don't: how long it will take us to get to all these places. That's why I asked you if the schedule was doable when I emailed it to you." I didn't bother to say that I could see that he'd read it, even though he hadn't responded. To any of my emails.

"Glad to know there's *something* I know that you

don't." This time, the smirk he let run free across his face was irresistible and bit the inside of my cheek, suddenly reconsidering my desire to keep this job. Or just my traitorous desire.

"Settle down. You're a doctor, remember? You know everything."

His green eyes bore holes through my own as I started to feel the weight of his gaze. Then, something amazing happened. A slow smile crawled across his face and a loud, guffawing laugh erupted out of him. It was a man's laugh, full bodied and deep. A little rusty, too. It went on for longer than I expected and I couldn't look away, a little turned on but more envious at how he just let himself fall into the laugh. It was a sight to see. "Ah, thanks for that Stevie."

"My pleasure, Doc."

"Scott. Call me Scott."

That didn't seem like a good idea. "Not very professional."

He shrugged. "Tulip is a small town and we don't much stand on ceremony, so call me Scott. I insist."

Well, if *he* insisted. "All right, Scott. I'm gonna go get some work done before we head out. Field work." I tried to put a little fear in my eyes, but I'd settle for worry. If Scott needed to think he could run me off, the victory would be so much sweeter when he asked me to stay.

SCOTT

e were headed to our third ranch of the day and, still, Stevie hadn't gone all girly on me. She hadn't complained when Tally licked her and her brand-new calf in one fell swoop, or when she fell butt-first into the dirt thanks to Bill Crane's overeager golden retrievers. She took every single one of them in stride. It was a relief compared to all my other assistants —especially Tori, who had been grossed about everything to do with animals. In general, women who chose to work in an office environment didn't do well outside of it.

Except Stevie.

So far, anyway. The Cullen Farm was up next, and it was an unconventional operation. If she could survive the Cullen place, then she would survive the rest—I just hadn't figured out whether I wanted her to or not, yet. "It's a good thing you don't dress for a conventional office." Showing up in jeans and sneakers made bringing her along an easy decision.

Stevie snorted in response to my attempt at conversation. I'd give her that, unlike so many of the other women I knew, she didn't talk nonstop. "If you have an office dress code, you should just say so." She turned towards me and I swear, her violet eyes bore a hole into the side of my face.

"Like I said, it's a good thing. Otherwise you would've been unbearable about being in the field today."

She didn't complain, which I appreciated more than I would ever share with her.

"You work with animals, yet *my* clothes are the problem?" Her gaze slid down my polo shirt, the only concession of my wardrobe to being out in the field, and then down to the beige khaki pants and my rubber-soled dressed shoes. "Right," she said, drawing the word out into three syllables, just in case there was any confusion on what *she* thought of my clothes.

"What's wrong with what I'm wearing?" I looked professional and casual.

"Absolutely nothing. If you're a pediatrician or one of those ENT guys. Don't you think you're a tad overdressed for sticking your arm up a cow's backside?" I couldn't tell if she was screwing with me or not—her ebony brows rested in a straight line just like her face, giving nothing away.

I looked down at my clothes and shook my head. "This is exactly how I should dress for field work."

She shrugged. "Okay."

"Okay? So suddenly you're just fine with my outfit?"

Stevie gave a fake shudder and shook her head. "Oh

22

no, I still think it screams magazine salesman…or worse. But it's your choice and, if nothing else, I respect that." She turned away from me, giving me a moment to watch her in profile. Her nose had a cute little upturn and her lips were thick and full, the top just a smidge fuller than the bottom. She turned back to me with a mischievous smile. "See how that worked right there? You explained yourself and even though I disagreed, I left it alone."

Once again, she managed to surprise a laugh out of me. "Anyone ever tell you you're a smartass?"

"Only every day of my life."

She smiled and, dammit, she was beautiful.

I shouldn't be thinking that way about an employee, and I *definitely* shouldn't be thinking that way about a woman I planned to fire in a few days. Maybe. Hopefully. "Why are you so comfortable around animals?" That was a safer topic of conversation.

"Can't I just be an animal lover?" she retorted quickly. I took my eyes off the road for a second to give her a look. "Okay, fine, I grew up on a farm. Nothing like the ones we've seen today, but there were enough animals that I'm comfortable around all types." I had a feeling she wasn't just talking about the four-legged creatures. "Disappointed I didn't freak out?"

"Kind of," I admitted. Stevie seemed to have a good read on people, which meant there was no point BS-ing her. "It is helpful to have an extra pair of hands, and it's better when you don't freak out about broken nails and new clothes."

"Then let's just consider my wardrobe a good thing and drop it?"

I laughed at her. As Eddy would say, Stevie had moxie. I might not completely hate having her as an assistant. "Well, thanks for your help," I told her as we pulled into the Cullen Farm.

"Just doing my job."

I appreciated that for her, it was as simple as that. But I'd been burned before, and I wouldn't make up my mind completely until I was sure. "Do you like horses?"

She shrugged. "They're all right. Big and majestic and all that."

I smiled to myself. Stevie was as tough as nails on top of everything else, which tap danced on my protective instinct for some reason. That was exactly why I didn't want an assistant. Meddling grandmothers were a pain I didn't have time to deal with right now, and I certainly didn't want to be responsible for another person on top of that.

"Wow." The word came out on an awe-filled sigh as she caught sight of the Four Horsemen, the name Brenda Cullen had given to the wild mustangs that roamed the property whenever they felt like it. "Now *those* are horses."

"They're just visitors. The Four Horsemen." I laughed when she glared at me. "It's the truth."

"Just when I thought there were no more pockets of weird in Texas, the people of Tulip surprise me yet again."

Before I could ask about that vague statement, Stevie was out of the truck and walking towards the fence, where even more animals came to greet the newcomer.

I gave her a moment with the animals while I got my bag together. It was a standard part of every visit, but I always had to prepare myself for the expectations that came with meeting people on their home turf. I let out a deep breath, almost ready to interact with more than the animals, when a voice startled me out of my thoughts.

"I thought you'd given up on assistants for a while?" I knew that husky twang anywhere. Brenda Cullen, all grown up but still five foot nothing of annoyance.

"Not my choice," I ground out, because to engage meant the conversation would never end. Ever. "And I don't want to talk about it."

"About what?" Stevie appeared on the other side of Brenda, a mischievous smile on her face. "Need some help, boss?"

As if I'd let her carry this heavy bag. "I got it, Stephanie."

Her violet stare would have stopped my heart, if such a thing was possible. She turned to Brenda. "Stevie Mattis. Dr. Henderson's temporary assistant."

"Temporary? That explains it. I was just askin' how you came to be," Brenda tossed in, throwing some twang on her deep Texas accent.

Stevie rolled her eyes. "How I came to be is a story for another time, but I was hired by his business partner. Eddy."

As expected, Brenda laughed loud and long, pulling Stevie towards the barn.

"No!"

"Yep. You should have seen the way he growled at me

when he found me behind the desk"—she gasped dramatically—"*working.*"

Another round of laughter went up and even my own lips twitched at the way she told the story. "Did he do that scowly thing with the clenched jaws?" Brenda pressed.

"This one?" Stevie narrowed her gaze and pushed her lips out, brooding like some movie star on a poster. "Oh, yeah, I didn't know what it was supposed to be, but I was hoping to keep the job."

"Of course," Brenda said, like they were old friends.

"I can hear you. Both of you." It was the most ridiculous thing I could have said but they clearly needed an interruption.

"At least we know your ears work, even if your brain doesn't." Brenda shook her head, too much delight shining in her blue eyes. "He's needed an assistant for the past twelve months, but the man is stubborn."

"I'm not stubborn."

"Yeah? Then how come the bill I received last night was the first one I've gotten in ten months?" She pulled an envelope from her back pocket and handed it to Stevie. "And doctors are supposed to be smart."

"And ranchers are supposed to be nice. Welcoming, even."

Brenda laughed. "They're also supposed to be men, so I'm bucking tradition in a lot of ways."

"No kidding," Stevie added. "This is the strangest farm I've ever seen. No offense."

"None taken. This is a sanctuary. We take farm animals that have been abused or neglected and let them live out their lives here on the land. Peaceful, except for the occasional petting zoo."

"Incredible. If you ever need volunteers, let me know."

"I'll hold you to that." Brenda whipped out her phone and pressed it against Stevie's. "Now you'll know which number to avoid if you change your mind."

"If I get a life before I leave town, I'll just let you know that I'm not interested."

I couldn't tell if there was actual stress in her voice or if I was just hearing things, so I kept my focus on the pregnant goat I was here to check out. For now, I was happy to listen and learn more about Stevie.

"How long are you in Tulip for?"

"Until the end of the week, for sure. After that, I haven't figured it out yet."

"You came all the way down here for a temporary job?"

I held my breath and waited, eyes closed, for Stevie to lay it all out there. "I had to leave my old job, anyway, and a week of pay is better than a week without."

"Was your boss one of those men who can't keep his hands to himself?"

I froze, listening. She hadn't said why she'd left her old job, and I hadn't given her much of a reason to open up, either.

"No, he just couldn't keep it in his pants. He slept with the nurse on staff, a pharmaceutical sales rep, and the janitor, and that was just in the office." Her voice was amused, but she couldn't hide the hurt deep in her voice.

"So you didn't sleep with him?"

"Nope. He was a nice guy—a family guy, I thought. But

when his wife found out, she made him clear his office of all female temptation just to make sure he stayed faithful. Apparently, he didn't tell her the janitor was a dude, otherwise I can't understand her logic."

Yep, there was anger and hurt there, and I couldn't say I blamed her. She'd lost her job through no fault of her own. And now it was about to happen again.

Her explanation had sent Brenda into another fit of giggles, giving me plenty of time to check out the other animals in peace. It wasn't exactly what I'd pictured, but it kept Brenda from poking her noise in my business and that was an added bonus.

STEVIE

Fifteen. That's how old I was the last time I
felt exhausted in the best way possible. I
know everyone usually thinks of sex when they think of a
good, satisfied kind of exhaustion, but for me it's always
been real physical labor. Even though I spent far too much
time closed inside a too-small car with the giant known as
Scott Henderson, it was a fun day. Holding animals
against my chest, cooing to the young ones when necessary—it was a good damn day and even if I didn't last
longer than the week, today was worth the experience.

After leaving the Cullen Farm, we headed to two more
properties where Scott did his thing, tending to a few
horses before we made our way back to the office well
after sundown.

As soon as I walked inside my hotel room, I locked the
door and kicked off my shoes before making a beeline
straight for the shower. It was hot as hell and the water
pressure was mediocre at best, but it helped wash away

the dirt and grime, the animal hair and the hay. All of it swirled down the drain as the small bathroom filled with steam and I stood there under the spray until I felt mostly human again.

Most of my belongings were still locked away in the moving truck I still couldn't unload but still had to buy an extra parking space for, not to mention the cost of the truck itself. All, very likely, for nothing. I didn't feel like blow drying my hair, so I let it air dry and slipped into a pair of flannel pole-dancing clown pants and a matching t-shirt, then fired up my laptop. I couldn't wait for Scott to decide whether or not to get rid of me; I needed to be proactive. I looked for jobs all over the country, confident now that I could live a good and happy life outside the state of Texas that had become my de facto home over the past few years.

Scott was a rule follower, not a maverick. How effective and proficient I was at my job would never trump his discomfort at having me around looking the way I did, so I blasted my resume out for more than an hour before a knock at the door pulled me from my mission. With a frown, I stood and went to the door. I didn't have any friends in town, which meant no impromptu visitors.

Through the peephole, I spotted Eddy and another woman with brown and silver hair, wearing a green and pink cowboy shirt. Eddy was a meddler, sure, but mostly harmless, so I opened the door. "Good evening, ladies. Can I help you with something?"

"No, but we can help you," Eddy said, shoving me aside as she entered without an invitation. "Betty here has a few leads on rentals in town. Apartment or house, whatever you need. Her new daughter works for the mayor, you know."

I'd heard at least half a dozen times—each of them from Eddy. "I'm not ready to start looking at rental units yet," I told her honestly. I wouldn't break Scott's confidence, but I wouldn't hold on to his secrets unnecessarily, either. "And I don't think I asked for this?"

"You didn't, but Tulip is a special little town—our own little slice of heaven—and we pride ourselves on welcoming newcomers and helping our neighbors out. With the hours you're keeping over at Scotty's place, I figured you haven't had time to nail down a place yet."

She was right. Sort of. Mostly. I would be looking already if my status as a resident of Tulip was more concrete, but it wasn't. "I haven't had time, but I'm not going to look until I'm sure I'm staying."

The two women shared a look I couldn't decipher, and I honestly wasn't sure I wanted to. Then Eddy turned to me with a frown. "You already took the job." She sounded offended, like she had been betrayed.

I nodded, because even though Tulip wasn't my hometown and I wasn't a proper Texas girl, I *was* raised to respect my elders. "And Dr. Henderson has instituted a probationary period for both of us." That was offering enough information without giving away all of it, right?

Betty folded her arms and dropped down on the bed —*my bed*—with a harrumph. "Sounds like a bunch of damn nonsense to me." She was a plainspoken woman with clear green eyes and a mind as sharp as a blade. "What's the truth, did your piercings scare him off?"

Absolutely. "I have no idea, he didn't say."

"Or the tattoos. My boy always did have an aversion to body art," Eddy added with a shake of her head, tracing the visible tip of the angel's wings that wrapped around the top of my shoulder.

"I said I have no idea, ladies, and I don't. I haven't asked and I won't. If my ability to do the job well doesn't land me this position for as long as I want it, nothing will. I'm fine with that. You should be, too." This was, by far, the strangest visit I'd ever had in my entire life. "Now, if you'll excuse me—"

"You're leaving?" Betty sounded hurt, which was strange since I'd only met her about three minutes ago. Maybe five, I didn't know—to me, it felt like a lifetime. "She's looking for a new job, Eddy. Look right here!" She pointed at my screen and Eddy dropped down beside her with the energy of a woman half her age.

"Why?"

Oh, she was good. She'd fooled me once and I could see, now, why she caused so much trouble for her strait-laced grandson. "I might not have a choice, Eddy. Especially since someone got me to pack up my life and move here under false pretenses." Eddy blushed but she looked directly at me, defiance burning in her eyes like she was an innocent woman.

"I gave you the shot you needed, don't blame me if you're determined to screw it all up."

I had to smile at her spirit. "I like you, Eddy. You're

crazy as hell and I dig that, but I need you to stop meddling. This is my life and my livelihood, and I need this job."

She scoffed and shook a hand in the air. "If that's the problem, I'll talk to Scotty—"

"No. Absolutely not. Please do not talk to Scott about me for any reason. Please," I added, just in case it might actually work.

After a long pause, she nodded. "Okay. Fine. I won't try to influence Scotty where your job is concerned. I promise." She crossed a finger over her heart and did her best to look like a woman with a lot less mischief in there.

It seemed too easy, but I was too tired to fight and I had a feeling these old ladies rarely lost. "Thank you."

They both shuffled out the door as easily as they'd pushed their way in, sighing as they turned to me. "There's a potluck dinner at the community center tomorrow. It's for charity," Betty added to entice me further.

Food and charity. There were worst ways to spend a night. "Do I have to dress up?"

Eddy looked me up and down. "It wouldn't kill you to wear something nice, but it's not required." They both gave me a long, assessing look before walking away.

I stood there, feeling like they'd walked away with everything they wanted and left me holding the bag.

SCOTT

*T*here was only one reason to get up early. Revenge. Sick, twisted revenge that harmed no one except the idiot crazy enough to get up an hour early just to beat his assistant to the office. Me, I'm that idiot. But it didn't matter—I woke up early, skipped my morning run and breakfast, and I made it in before Stevie arrived.

It was damned annoying to see her scowling face lit by the light of the computer screen every single morning. She never smiled at me, just hopped up and retrieved my coffee and messages. Every single morning. Like clock-work. But that morning, I'd beat her in, and I damn sure wasn't going to waste the time.

First, I logged onto the system to check out the new filing system, which was a lot. Too much, in fact. It was overly complicated and I didn't know where anything was, which meant she would have to redo it. I smiled, just thinking of how mad she would be when I gave her that news. Sometime just before nine, I heard Stevie enter the office. She paused, briefly, before falling easily into her morning routine.

Unflappable as ever. I was determined to see the woman get annoyed. Or angry.

Ten minutes later, she breezed in with a big steaming mug of coffee and a familiar white bag, soaked with grease at the bottom. She set both items on the corner of my desk, then stepped back and waited before she turned and left without a word.

Strange.

Stevie's confidence in her abilities as an assistant was warranted, which is why her sudden silence was so bothersome. Was she planning on leaving before I made a decision? Had she already checked out?

I didn't know—not yet—but she was efficient as heck, making my life far easier than thought it could be. I had already accepted that this life as a small-town vet would be harder than that of my counterparts who treated the sick pets of the rich and famous, since I had to pull triple duty as doctor, nurse, and administrator. But Stevie had, somehow, made things much simpler in the few days she'd been around. Hot, refreshed coffee regularly appeared on my desk, and so far, there had been no double-booked appointments, forgotten meetings, or any other trouble.

It was all smooth sailing. It almost felt too smooth.

Another knock sounded, pulling me from my thoughts and from the mountain of paperwork I needed to approve now that the filing system was officially up to date and online. The stack in front of me was filled with invoices, old and new, along with equipment orders, lab fees to be paid, and plenty of other admin stuff I'd been neglecting under the guise of doing it all myself. "Come in," I barked, annoyed at the interruption even though I knew exactly who it was.

Stevie appeared on the other side of my desk in another pair of painted on blue jeans and a short-sleeved T-shirt that was not workplace appropriate. It wasn't revealing, it'd need a few more inches to come close, but it was still low-key sexy. She dropped another bag on my desk and took a step back. "Your first appointment after lunch is at one-fifteen. A Doberman with a bowel problem, belongs to Martha Clark."

I groaned. Martha was the kind of pet owner who fed her dog human food, non-stop, ignoring all dietary orders she was given. "Thanks." She gave a short nod and turned on her heels. "Wait."

Stevie turned, slowly, pushing a mass of curls out of her face. "Yes?"

"What's this?" A dumb question, I knew, but we were both aware of what I was really asking.

"Lunch. People generally eat it between breakfast and dinner. You don't want it?"

"I do," I insisted, even though I wasn't sure if I really did. "What is it?"

Stevie shrugged and leaned against the doorframe with a casual ease I envied most days. "Burger and fries. Figured it was a safe bet."

I frowned, wondering what her angle was but aware

that asking about it might just piss her off. "What did you get?"

"Nachos. Loaded with extra jalapeño and guac." She flashed a proud smile and I groaned.

"That sounds heavenly."

"It does, and it's mine. You have a burger and fries," she reminded me, chin tilted up, defiant.

My lips twitched at her attempt at putting her foot down, which I allowed. "Thank you for lunch, Stevie."

"You're welcome," she said softly and left my office.

She also left me confused, but that wasn't on her. It was on me and my unbelievable reaction to this woman who wasn't my type. Not even a little bit.

My phone lit up with Derek's face as it began to ring and I smiled, reaching for it. I needed to talk to someone about these strange, protective feelings she was stirring in me, but if I talked to Derek, newly in love, he would undoubtedly see things that weren't there.

"Derek, how goes the business of overcharging clients?"

"I don't know, you tell me. How much is a doggy massage going for these days?" The amusement in his voice soothed his words, even though neither of us meant them.

"You couldn't afford one," I shot back with a laugh.

"So, how is the assistant going? I heard she has a ring in her nose, is it true?"

I nodded, turning to look out at the view of the fields of tulips on the other side of the window. "It is true, a light purple stone that almost matches her eyes." Shit, why did I say that? "She also has a row of earrings all the way up one ear." That was better, a perfect distraction.

"Are you freaking out? I bet you're freaking out right now, and counting down the days until you can fire her, aren't you?" Derek laughed again, so confident he knew me and I had to admit, as my best friend, he really did.

"I'm not freaking out." There was no need to, not when the end of the week was just around the corner and I was, unfortunately, no closer to a decision than I'd been the day she called me on already having my mind made up. "She's efficient," I added weakly.

"That's a good thing. So, what is it about this woman that has you so unsure?"

"I don't know," I admitted, even though I had *some* idea. "She brought me lunch. Double bacon cheeseburger with fries." What in the hell did that mean, anyway? Was she sucking up to the boss, or did she get it because I always work through lunch?

Derek was quiet for a long minute and I strained to see if there were any sounds of an impending emergency. "She doesn't sound like your type, even though Betty swears she's as pretty as a picture."

"Your point?"

"My point is, what would be the harm in keeping her on for awhile?"

The harm was that Stevie was absolutely not my type, but that didn't mean she lacked a certain appeal. She was attractive and mouthy, and that wild black hair made my fingers itch to run through it. Dammit.

"I don't know." That was the honest-to-god truth.

Silence descended on the other end of the line, for so long I was about to hang up, when Derek spoke. "You like her."

"She's my assistant. Very capable, what's not to like?" Why was he reading more into this than there actually was?

"And you *like* her. As a human, maybe even as a person." He laughed, so damn amused by himself. "Then I guess you'd better get used to having her around, because it sounds like you couldn't get rid of her even if you really wanted to—and you don't sound like a man who's ready to see the back of this woman." He laughed again. "Or maybe you want to see much more than the back of her."

"I didn't say I was keeping her," I barked angrily, but Derek didn't find me the least bit intimidating.

"Good," he snorted, "because she isn't a pet. She's a woman. An employee."

Which meant she was off-limits no matter what feelings she stirred up inside me. "Did you call just to give me shit?" It was exactly the kind of thing we did, but not so much since he'd started spending every free moment with Max and Callie.

"No, I actually called for a reason. Giving you shit was just a bonus." He rifled through some papers and when he spoke again, I heard the smile in his voice. "The Hometown Heroes potluck mixer is tomorrow night. Bring a homemade dish and your best smile."

"Shit. Will this ever end?"

"Probably not, but those old ladies helped me land Maxine, so I can't complain too much."

"You complained plenty while it was happening, believe me." And as amusing as it had been to watch, it had also been kind of painful. Some things, a man needed to do himself.

"Maybe so, but I've got my woman now, which means more women to focus on your pathetic love life." This time, I heard the muffled sounds of the speaker and I reached for my lunch.

"Gotta go. Talk to you later, and good luck with the assistant."

"Stevie. Her name is Stevie."

Derek sighed. "There is something sexy about a woman with a man's name." With that, the call was over and I groaned—instead of relaxing at home tonight, I had to cook something.

For charity.

And I was pretty sure it would be inappropriate to pass it off onto my assistant.

Right?

STEVIE

Standing outside a small-town community center on a Friday night with a chilly bowl of Bloody Mary dip in my arms was not how I'd imagined spending my night. But here I was, staring nervously at the imposing white stone structure that seemed out of place in this small town, scrambling for the courage to go inside.

I hadn't ever been much of a "joiner" throughout my life. Not when it came to the clothing drive in high school —I'd just slipped two bags of old clothes into the truck at the end of the school day—and not when it came to any other group activity. I much preferred binge-watching TV shows from the comfort of my own home, wherever that was at any given moment. But, somehow, I'd let two old ladies convince me to not only make a dish, but to show up in person.

"She didn't dress up like Eddy told her to, but she's a pretty little thing." The voices came from behind me, and even though I didn't want to turn, I had to. Two very different older women were staring at me. One with dark exotic features, and the other with fair skin and graying hair. Opposites attract seemed to be the theme of these friendships.

"She doesn't speak very much, does she?" The question came from the fair-skinned woman.

"I speak enough," I told them. "But it's not every day that two random strangers start talking about me like they know me."

The dark-haired woman arched a brow. "She's got spunk, I like her."

"Yeah, I like her attitude, too. The name is Helen Landon, and this here is Elizabeth Vargas. Some of Tulip's finest, if you don't mind my saying."

"Nice to meet you both. I assume you round out the *Sex & the City* foursome with Eddy and Betty?"

"Oh, I like that," Helen said. "I'll be the blond one, she's sassy."

"Slutty, you mean," Elizabeth amended. "You'd have to get out a little more just to be slutty."

"I get out just fine," she retorted, feigning hurt. "We're not here to talk about me, anyway. Let's get Stevie inside and introduce her around."

"Oh, that won't be necessary," I told them, even as both women stood on either side of me and basically herded me into the building, like cattle. "I can find my way, myself."

"Just go with it, honey," Elizabeth whispered. "This is how we do things and it'll go easier if you just go along."

That really wasn't my strong suit.

"Stevie here has brought a dish," Helen announced, speaking like I was a special charity project. "Isn't she just lovely?"

A few older women who had gathered around the table half-filled with homemade dishes nodded and smiled. One even leaned in and pinched my cheek. "Beautiful. Even if she doesn't do a damn thing to help herself," Betty said from behind me.

"Eddy said dressing up was an option, and it's an option I didn't want to consider." Why I was explaining myself, I didn't know. Maybe it was being surrounded by half a dozen women who were professional moms. "What's the big deal? This is for charity, right?"

"Of course," Elizabeth said and took the bowl from my hands. "But it never hurts to put in a little effort."

"I'm not looking to hook up right now." There was no point in letting these women think they could get their little miss matchmaker on with me when I wasn't looking.

"That's the best time to find exactly what you need," Betty assured me with a sympathetic smile that said she knew they were all a bit much.

"Thanks for the kind words and everything, but really, I just came to offer some help and see what this small-town thing was all about." I'd be gone soon enough, so there was no point in letting them get close or starting to like them—even though they were the pushiest, funkiest, most bad-ass old ladies I'd ever come across in my travels through this great state.

"At least smile. You have such great teeth." Helen

grinned at me as if the problem was that I didn't know how to smile, not that I didn't want to. "Better. A little bigger would be better, though."

I rolled my eyes. "Do you serve alcohol at these things?"

Eddy laughed and wrapped an arm around my waist, pulling me into her bony frame. "I think I've found my new best friend. Let me show you where the cold beer is kept."

"Bless you, Eddy." I let her tear me away from the rest of the women, sucking in a deep breath when we arrived at the drinks table, which held far fewer people in general and a lot fewer matchmaking matrons.

"Even dressed like a teenage boy, you're a knockout. That should help. Have fun tonight—and use condoms." Then, like she hadn't just said *what she'd just said*, Eddy sauntered back to her circle of friends, all of whom turned to stare at me.

I turned away, taking Eddy's advice for the ice cold beer and finding a table that looked like it hadn't been claimed yet. It was close to the exit and slightly shielded by the overbearing decorations. I didn't know what the Hometown Heroes were—or rather, *who*—but they had one hell of a marketing campaign. The tribute, even in its current state, was a beautiful monument to another bad-ass woman, another reason I was happy to attend tonight.

"You're new." A woman with dark hair and a slightly rounded pregnant belly stood in front of me, sizing me up and looking amused about it.

"I am. Temporary, too."

She grinned. "I'm Nina. I was the new girl earlier this year."

"Not so new anymore," I pointed out, nodding towards her belly.

"Not at all." She laughed and rubbed her belly the way pregnant women tended to do. "Why are you over here all alone?"

"Because those old ladies were a little too interested in my appearance." I sounded grumpy, and I kind of was. And, yeah, it *was* kind of nice to have people fuss over me, but it was still weird.

She laughed. "That's the matchmaking crew. Who are they trying to match you with?"

"No one." It was a rookie mistake to answer so quickly. I knew that, and apparently, Nina did, too.

"What did you say you were doing in town?"

"I didn't."

Another woman, a redhead, laughed. "Okay. What brings you to town?"

I sighed. "I came here for a job, but it ends soon. Then, I'll be gone." That much was true. I'd finished up at the office, and Scott hadn't said one word to me. The. Whole. Day. It didn't take a genius to figure out, so I'd left the office and threw the key through the mail slot before heading back to my room.

"Eddy mentioned something about finding an assistant for Scott. Her name was cutesy, like a boy's name."

"Stevie," I grunted. "That's me. Stevie."

"I'm Penny, this is Max, and that's Nina. Welcome to Tulip."

"Thanks. Nice to meet you all."

They all sat, dashing my hopes that they were just passing by. "Why are you leaving so quickly?"

"A girl's gotta work, and the work here suddenly dried up." Each time I said it, the words went down a little easier.

"So, you're going home, then?" That came from Max.

"No. There is no home, but I'll go somewhere and that will be home." Each of the women looked at me like I said I killed kittens for fun. "It's no big deal. My mom's dead and my dad lives in New Zealand with his new family. I might head west. Or east. I haven't decided yet."

Another round of silence bounced around the table, and I sighed. This was why I didn't get attached to people —the weight of their expectations was too much to carry along with my own.

"Then you can stay here." That was Penny, and I didn't get why it mattered to her. Or any of them.

"Except I don't have a job, and there's not even a job board in this town." Which meant that either there were no jobs, or they were all given out based on who you knew—and I knew no one.

Three sets of eyes stared at me for about a minute and then, one by one, they stood with a smile and a sad shake of their heads before leaving. It was weird as hell, and suddenly I was a little less sad about packing up and moving on this weekend.

But the people of Tulip were very interesting to watch.

The older ladies I'd met earlier still gathered around the food table, only now their attention was on a group of men I assumed were the Hometown Heroes. They were all good looking, almost *too* good looking, and casting wary glances right back at the women. A few of the guys wore big, amused smiles and the rest looked miserable. And worried.

I soaked up as much of the small-town atmosphere as I could, watching who flirted with whom, who casted longing glances and who snuck off seconds after someone else. It was amusing and it made me just the teensiest bit sad I wouldn't be around to observe more.

"What are you doing here?"

I froze at the sound of Scott's voice beside me. It was a reminder of why I didn't let myself get too carried away. Anyone could sneak up on you. "Last I checked, this was still a free country and I can go wherever I like."

He let out a weary sigh and though I refused to look at him, I caught a glimpse of his sagging shoulders. "I just meant that I didn't realize you were getting involved."

"Hardly involved," I snorted. "I brought a dish to a charity potluck, I'm not buying a house and running for office." This town was as nosy as all the dime-store romance novels suggested. When it wasn't aimed at me, it was kind of amusing, but being on the other end of Scott's stare was less so.

"I didn't realize."

"Why would you? It's not like we're friends or anything. Look." I turned to him, which was a really bad idea because the heated look in his green eyes just about

47

scorched the panties right off my body. "Look, I'm enjoying one night in this town and then I'm gone, all right? Not that it's any of your business, anyway."

He frowned in response but his lips were like granite, never moving from that dissatisfied and disapproving flat line.

I stood, suddenly bored with this conversation. "Have a nice life, Dr. Henderson." The drinks were cold and, if nothing else, the old ladies were friendly, so I gave myself a half hour. If things didn't pick up, I would turn in early for an even earlier departure.

I didn't have to turn around to know he was on my heels; his body was so damn big it had its own gravitational field. Next to him, I was no match.

"I'm sorry. I should have done more to make you feel welcome."

I laughed and reached into the pink cooler for an icy beer before turning to Scott. "It's not your responsibility to make me feel anything other than appreciated in the workplace, and even there I'd settle for mere civility. But that still seems to be too much for you, and that's fine. I work for you. That's all—and even that has an expiration date." The last thing I needed at this point in my life was someone to suddenly start giving a damn and poking into my life. No, thank you.

"That's now how things work around here, Stevie. We look after each other—to an almost annoying degree, in fact."

That managed to pull another laugh out of me. "I've noticed, but I'm not from around here and you don't need to babysit me. I can handle the old ladies, *and* the newly married ones, too." I nodded to the group of men, still congregated in the same spot, only their handsome numbers had grown. "Go have fun with your friends. It seems like you don't spend much time away from your office."

"I could say the same about you."

"That's true, with the small exception being that I don't know anyone in this town, which means I don't have anything else to do but work. You were born and raised here, according to Eddy."

"You got me there." His smile was softer this time, more genuine and wistful. "Growing my business has been hard, and I'm wondering if my aversion to assistants has made it harder than it needed to be." He raked a hand through his hair and laid a grin on me that had me weak in the knees and grateful I was sitting down. And wearing leather boots with *no* heels.

"You'll figure it out." Or he wouldn't. Tomorrow was my last day at the office and on Saturday morning, this town—adorable and weird though it was—would be firmly in my rearview mirror.

"You don't know that."

"Nope, I don't. But you probably do." I knocked back half the beer and smacked my lips together. It was cold and had just enough alcohol in it to give me the warm-and-tingleys. "Have a good night."

"Where you off to in such a hurry?" Eddy stood right in my path. Her lips matched the bright pink jumpsuit she wore.

"I'm off to... anywhere else. See ya around, Eddy." I put a hand on her shoulder and her bony but surprisingly strong fingers wrapped around my wrist.

"Not before taking a twirl on the dance floor. Scotty, ask the woman to dance."

Scott blinked, looking even more stunned than I felt, which left me feeling oddly offended. "Actually, I'm off to the bathroom," I said inanely, rushing off as fast as my legs would carry me. This town was getting stranger by the minute and as soon as I took a breath, I was getting the hell away from matchmakers and cranky, but sexy veterinarians.

"He'd better watch out, 'cause I'm sure they're already looking for a woman for him." Conversation stopped when I pushed the door open and I froze.

"Sorry, I just needed a... minute."

The blond smiled wide at me and the two brunettes wore more reserved smiles. "It's okay, that's why we're all in here. Who are you running from?"

"Don't mind Hope, she doesn't realize that not everyone is happy to share every moment of their lives with the entire town." She stuck her hand out. "Bo."

"You run the general store. You have the best snacks."

Her smile was wider this time. "Good to know. This is Hope and that's Mikki, she was new until you arrived."

"Hey. I'm Stevie."

"Scott's Stevie?" The blond, Hope, asked with big hope-filled eyes.

"No, just Stevie." It was official, the whole damn town was crazy. "I'll just be... in here." I made my escape to one of the stalls, but the silence now made it awkward.

"I know you don't know us, and if you know Eddy, you probably think we're crazy as hell." That matter of fact voice had to be the one called Bo. "But do not underestimate the old ladies."

The other two laughed. "I know the serious tone seems a little over the top, but she's right. You and Scott might not seem like a good match on the surface—"

"Hope, that's rude."

"Mikki, I'm just trying to be honest with her before she runs outta here thinkin' she's free." Hope knocked on the door. "Stevie, can you just come out, because this door is the ugliest shade of blue ever created and you're not even doing anything in there."

She was right and even though it was very clean, it was still a public restroom. "Fine. But I don't need a lecture because I'm out of here as of Saturday morning."

"You sure?" Bo folded her arms and arched a brow but it was all for show, to let me know I shouldn't be so sure.

"That was the deal and, unless I hear otherwise, I'm gone then."

"Excellent." Bo clapped her hands together and jumped off the sink. "Then you can do what you like. But if I were you, I'd keep an eye on them until you have the Welcome to Tulip sign behind you. Those old biddies somehow got me to fall in love with my best friend." Her smile softened, but her disbelief was real. And new.

"I appreciate the warning and I promise to be careful."

"It's not about being careful," she went on, invading my

personal space. "Just stay away from Scott. The more they can see it, the more convinced they'll be that they're right."

"She's right," Mikki added with a shrug. "They're crafty."

"I know. Eddy got me here under false pretenses." I wasn't all that upset about it; I really hated job hunting.

"That sucks. I have one part-timer and so does Mikki. Hope just started her own lingerie business, and you don't look like the retail sort."

"I'm not, but thanks anyway." Yep, this town grew weirder by the second and I was determined to enjoy as much of it as I could before I drove away and this town became like all the others—just a memory.

SCOTT

I'm just here to say goodbye. That's what I told myself when I killed the engine in the parking lot of the hotel where Stevie had been staying all week. It was barely a hotel, probably not even a motel. Hell, I didn't even know this place was part of Tulip and I didn't imagine most other people did either, or else it wouldn't have escaped the recent town improvement initiatives. This place was a hellhole—and that was putting it nicely. The only saving grace was that there was very little crime in Tulip.

"Say goodbye and get going." That was the plan, and I was sticking to it. I'd spent all week thinking about what to do about the Stevie situation and, until the potluck dinner, I had planned to ask her to stick around. But Eddy and the others clearly had me and Stevie in their sights, which meant it was best for her to move on.

"Hey."

Stevie looked up from packing with a blank expression on her face. "Hey. What's up?" She was just so matter-of-fact as she packed up her life. Again.

Shit. I hated seeing her like this, all resigned and disappointed, but unwilling to show it. It was almost like she'd been expecting this very outcome from the beginning, which just pissed me off. Not only that she thought she knew me, but also because it meant I was exactly who she had accused me of being—someone who couldn't see past who she was on the surface. "Going somewhere?"

"Yep." She spared me exactly one second for a look before zipping up the small bag on the edge of her bed. "Headed out on the last train out of town."

My brows crinkled in confusion. Was this some type of gag, or was she seriously talking like a cowboy from the old west? "Why?"

"Hard to find jobs in small towns. It's why no one ever moves to'em." There was an edge in her voice that hadn't been there before.

"You already have a job."

She shook her head immediately; there wasn't a moment of joy or hope. Just disbelief. "As of five o'clock yesterday, my temporary employment expired, so I'm headed off to find my fortune elsewhere."

"What?"

Stevie stopped and looked at me again, annoyance the only emotion on her face. "Was there some word in there you didn't understand?"

"No." I blinked, feeling like the conversation had changed when I wasn't looking.

"Okay, then." She lifted a box onto the bed and

rearranged its contents before folding it shut and lifting it once more to set it down beside the open door. When her petite frame unfolded, the top of her head didn't even reach my chin and I smirked, which she did not appreciate. "Was there something else?"

No. That was what I should have said. Instead, a whole different set of words tumbled out of my mouth. "The job is yours. For as long as you want it." If I had been expecting gratitude or happiness, I would have been disappointed.

She folded her arms over her chest and glared at me. "Why?"

"You're good at your job and you don't annoy me. Much. Plus, those extra hands on field days really help a lot." I wiggled my fingers and she laughed, rolling her eyes at me. "Good enough reasons?"

"As long as this has nothing to do with Eddy or the others."

"None at all," I assured her.

"Thanks. I think I'll take you up on that job offer." She smiled and held out her hand until I took it, my own hand swallowing hers up in the process. "I appreciate the personal touch, but you could have just called."

She was right, I could have called, but I needed to see her. To make sure she was all right with how things were supposed to play out, I had told myself, but now I knew why I really came. To force myself to do the right thing. "I know, but I have something else I wanted to discuss with you."

She backed up, suddenly uneasy. "I'm not taking a pay cut," she insisted. Again.

"What the hell is it with you and pay cuts?" She really had an issue about it.

"I know how bosses operate. *'It's just for a week, Stevie. We'll be all caught up at the end of the month. Just to get us through this rough period,'*" she said, voice pitched low in the tone of her male bosses. "I've heard it enough to know that it's best to be up-front about these things."

I accepted that, thinking how much human garbage she must have come across in her young life to be so cynical. So tough. "It's about your, uh, living arrangements." That was sloppy, and I didn't blame her for the outrage gaining steam in her violet eyes.

She stood a little taller and let her hands drop to her sides, balling into fists before unballing them, and then balling them right back up again. She always looked so tough in her trademark jeans and T-shirts that showed off toned arms. And tattoos. "What about them?"

"I have a guest house. Actually, it's more like a carriage house."

She held up a hand. "Neither of those words mean a thing to me."

"The carriage house is a smaller house located on my property, and it's unoccupied at the moment. Plus, it's about a quarter mile, give or take, from my house. If you're interested." That was clumsy as hell, and I wouldn't be surprised if she said no on principle alone. But housing wasn't cheap and I knew how much she made.

"I'm not sleeping with you to keep my job, Scott."

What will get you to sleep with me? I couldn't ask her that, of course, especially minutes after offering her a job. But there was no harm in thinking it, was there? "If we're going to work together, Stevie, you'll need to work on your negativity."

"What negativity? It's pragmatism, that's all."

I laughed at her quick wit. Even if she was a little more tempting than I'd like, her smart mouth would ensure we stayed nothing but friends. "If that's what you need to believe, sure. But sleeping with me is not part of your work contract or your rental agreement. Got it?"

She nodded. "How much?"

I quoted her the same price as the last tenant and her violet eyes went round in surprise.

"Then you've got yourself an assistant." Relief showed on her face, but I had a feeling it would take months, maybe longer, before she got comfortable around here.

"Excellent. You want to drop your stuff off at the carriage house, or get a celebratory drink at Black Thumb?"

She snorted a laugh. "You guys really go all out with this whole flower theme, don't ya?"

I picked up the box and took it to the truck parked right in front of her room. "This town likes to be consistent, and themes are the kind of consistency that tourists appreciate. And we appreciate tourist dollars."

She nodded, a mischievous tilt to her lips. "What do the tourists have to say about beer at the Black Thumb?"

"It's ice cold, and the food is good and greasy." She didn't seem to be a prissy kind of girl, another strike against her being my type, because I preferred my women on the extreme side of girly. Stevie was the opposite—a grownup tomboy, really.

"Now you're just trying to butter me up." She lifted her two bags and strode to the truck, jumping inside and moving around capably. More than someone her size should be able to.

"Need a hand?"

"I got it. Just drive a little on the slow side, since I don't know where I'm going and this town is so Podunk even my GPS can't get around." She wasn't just a tomboy, no—it was worse. Stevie was a curmudgeon. "What's so funny?"

"You. You're like a grumpy old man. It's hilarious."

She narrowed her violet gaze at me and jumped down from the truck, yanking the sliding door down with her. "You're not funny, and don't think that I'm gonna laugh because you're my boss."

"Of course not. You'll laugh because I'm funny as hell." Her lips twitched, but her iron will wouldn't let the smile win. "The time will come. I'm not worried."

"Neither am I." She gave me a long look, licked her lips and turned to get in her car.

"Who's driving the truck?"

"Me. After I hitch it to my car. Duh."

I shook my head at this crazy woman, thankful she was an excellent assistant and even more thankful she wasn't my type.

So very thankful.

STEVIE

"*I*'ll have a shot of tequila and your best brown ale." Just because I agreed to have a drink with Scott, my boss, didn't mean I would let him buy my drinks. The guy was already giving me a pretty good deal on rent—okay, it was a damn good deal—and the last thing I needed was to feel indebted to him. "And two pitchers for the rowdy bunch in the back."

The owner, Buddy, who I'd been introduced to earlier, leaned on the bar with his forearms exposed, flannel sleeves pushed up to just below his elbows. "What are you doing with the likes of them?"

"Isn't it obvious? I'm drinking." At least I would be as soon as the tap finished filling up my glass.

"You know what you're doing?"

It was sweet of this big gruff man to be worried about me. He didn't know me from Adam but his concern was kind of sweet, which should really be the tagline for this town. "I'll be all right. Most of them are taken, and I'm not looking. Unless you know something I don't?"

"Plenty, I reckon, but they're all good boys. You're safe, anyway."

That was good enough for me. I wasn't worried about my safety or my virtue, because I could take care of myself, and since I wasn't looking for a man or even a bed warmer right now, none of us had anything to worry about. As soon as Buddy slid the glass my way, I knocked it back and took a sip of beer. Now I was ready to face the big group of handsome Hometown Heroes.

"Wish me luck."

"I wouldn't dare. The wrong ears could be listening and misinterpret it." Buddy's smile was warm, but something about it caused a knot of worry to form in my gut. I couldn't explain it, other than to say that some of the people in Tulip had clearly gotten in my head.

Luckily for me, carrying two pitchers of beer plus my own tall glass required all of my concentration, so I didn't have time or brain space to waste on things I couldn't control.

"Okay, boys, beer. As promised."

"I like her already." Nate relieved me of one of the pitchers and his brother Jase grabbed the other. "Thanks, Stevie."

"No problem." I took the seat at the end of a long table, across from Scott and next to his friend Derek. "So, who wants to fill me in on the whole Hometown Heroes thing?"

Silence descended and then all six guys started talking at once. "I can't believe you didn't tell her."

"Basically, it means we're sex symbols." That came from Will, a handsome paramedic with gorgeous gray eyes.

Nate elbowed Will in the side. "It's a calendar. For charity, to help rebuild Tulip's Tribute without Preston's mom getting her rich hands all over it." I didn't know what most of that meant, so I just nodded.

"Okay. And you're heroes because of your jobs, or for stepping up to be naked for charity?"

Scott spat his beer out, spraying everyone at the table. "What the hell, Stevie? We're not naked!"

I shrugged. "Too bad, because that's a calendar I would pay good money for. I mean, you guys are handsome, but tell me you're at least shirtless?" I looked around at each of them, easily picking out who was brave enough, or would easily gave in to the photographer. "Interesting."

Jase frowned. "No one said anything. What's so interesting?"

"How many of you agreed to take your shirts off for a good cause. It's admirable. Really, it is." I tried to hold in the smirk, but they were all shifting in their seats and looking wildly uncomfortable, and I couldn't help messing with them. I raised my glass in the air. "To charity and the do-gooders that make the rest of us look bad."

"Cheers!" They were loud and boisterous, and these men didn't mind having a good time. The drinks flowed along with conversation and I got to know a little about each of the men. They were all flirts, even the ones who couldn't stop talking about the women who owned their hearts. They loved to give each other crap and—it seemed to me, anyway—they had each other's backs.

It was so damn sweet it almost gave me a toothache. But it was also kind of awesome and comforting, too. "What are you thinking about, I wonder?" Nate's red brows arched in curiosity as several men left the table when a group of women walked in.

"Nothing in particular. How nice it must be to work and hang around with your best friends."

He grunted. "It's nice, but don't let tonight fool you. We meddle, we push and we fight like hell. Most of the time we want to kill each other, but somehow, it all works out okay in the end."

That was a nice sentiment, one I wasn't all that familiar with. "I'll have to take your word for it." I nodded over his shoulder to one of the dark-haired women from the community center bathroom. "There's a beautiful brunette trying to get your attention."

A smile lit up his face, turning him from gruff to gorgeous in a flash. "That's Mikki."

"Well, don't keep her waiting." To his credit, Nate hesitated for a second about leaving me alone before he pushed away from the table and took long strides towards his woman. I watched, like the outsider I was, as he wrapped her in his arms and kissed her like they were alone. Like no one else was watching.

Then again, no one else was, because they were all busy with friends and loved ones. Everyone but me, anyway. So, I did what any sad sack did when surrounded by throngs of happy, coupled up people. "Buddy, another shot and a beer, please."

"Make it two and put it on my tab." I knew that voice better than any but my own, at this point.

"No need. I can pay for my own drinks, but you can stay if you want." No point in letting the boss think he could push me around when I was off the clock.

"Of course you can, but the offer was real. A welcome-to-Tulip shot and beer." He flashed his handsome, boyish grin, one I was sure made him irresistible to both young and old ladies alike. Even this lady, a little.

I rolled my eyes at his attempt to be cute. "Fine, you can buy me this shot and this drink. No more."

Scott held his hands up in defeat, the look of innocence on his face nowhere near believable. "I wouldn't dream of offending you by offering to buy you more than two drinks."

"One drink," I clarified. "Everyone knows a shot and a beer together are one drink. Right, Buddy?"

The gruff bartender nodded as he set our drinks in front of us and gave a shrug before ambling down to the other end of the bar to serve a few new arrivals.

"See?" I said. "Buddy knows what's up."

He gave me a half smile that said he was amused by me, and I didn't know whether to be flattered or annoyed by that. "You're a strange cookie, Stevie, you know that?"

"I do, but it's always nice to hear." He let out a low chuckle of amusement and I let the sound bounce off me, pretending it didn't have my blood vibrating at a molecular level. "You don't have to keep me company, Scott."

He shrugged. "I know."

Okay, then. "I don't need to be kept company."

"Neither do I." He turned to face me and I kept my gaze steady on the wall of booze behind the bar, refusing to give in to the discomfort that his interrogating stare caused. "A booth just opened up. I'll answer embarrassing questions about myself if you will."

I turned to him, a slow smile curling my lips. "I don't *do* embarrassing." His shoulders fell and I smacked another bill on the bar. "Another round of shots please, Buddy. But I'll answer personal questions for the chance to find one that embarrasses you."

His lips twitched as he stood and motioned for me to follow him. "I'll keep that in mind, but why don't we start simple. Where are you from?"

"All over Texas," I replied quickly. He arched his brows at me, knowingly. "Fine, I was born and raised on a small farm in Gary, Indiana. Then I grew up on a farm in Lubbock. After that, we moved around a lot." There wasn't much to tell, but I could tell it wouldn't satisfy his curiosity. "Dad sold the farm shortly after Mom died, convinced a woman couldn't do the job. We moved a lot after that." That wasn't the whole story, but it was all he would get and, thankfully, Scott was able to take a hint.

"I'm from Tulip," he offered easily.

Too easily. "No kidding. Were you raised by Eddy?"

Scott shook his head, but a wistful smile spread across his face. "Yes and no. I spent a lot of time with Eddy because my parents traveled a lot. Dad is an equine specialist and Mom is a rodeo coach. When it became clear I wasn't going to work with horses, they agreed I needed to focus more on my studies. Eddy was happy to have me."

"I'll bet. She's kooky as hell but, man, I bet she gets stuff done." She managed to get me here and someone keep Scott from firing me without even showing her face in the office once this past week.

"That's a pretty grown-up decision for a kid to make." Maybe he wasn't as golden as I thought.

"It was either that or choose something made me unhappy."

That surprised me. "You seem more of the *go-along-to-get-along* type, just to keep the peace." I could see Scott grinning and bearing it, just because he thought it was the right thing to do. "Color me surprised."

"You think I'd choose to be miserable?" He snorted a laugh. "You really do have a bad opinion of me."

"Not miserable, per se, but I think you'd do something that didn't satisfy you under the guise of doing the right thing. Whatever that is."

"Maybe you're right about that, I don't know. Siblings?"

I blinked at the quick topic change. "A couple step-siblings, maybe more. I'm not really sure." I hadn't spoken to my dad in years and the last time I did, he hadn't been able to stop talking about the newest addition to his family. *His*, not ours. "You?"

He barked out a laugh. "It's just me and my older

brother Tyson, he's the sheriff. My parents didn't spend enough time together to make me a big brother, too." He grinned but I could see the disappointment still swimming in his eyes.

"But they both work with horses."

"Yes, but dad works on Olympic horses, dressage and all that, while mom is a rodeo girl." He smiled easily when he talked about his parents, but the tension never left his eyes or mouth, giving away his truest, most deeply-held feelings about his parents.

"Impressive." I stared at him and remembered the old ladies. "Never married?"

"Nope. You?"

"Nope. Why not?"

He shrugged. "Vet school took up most of my time and, in case you haven't noticed, I grew up with most of the women in this town. They're either good friends of mine or my parents'."

That would make dating hard and getting some nookie downright impossible, unless you were creative. "Bummer for you."

"You don't have to worry about me, Stevie."

I blinked innocently. "I would never, ever dream of worrying about a doctor. They know everything, they'll be fine." I blinked and he laughed and the sound was deep and rich, like expensive chocolate.

I had to suppress a shiver.

"Good. Glad we understand each other." Scott flagged Buddy down and I realized more than a couple empty bottles and shot glasses now littered the table. "Why the tattoos?"

"Each one means something to me. A struggle or fight or success. Some people document with photos and souvenirs, I do it with body art." His gaze seemed less bothered by it now and more… I don't know, curious, I guess.

"I never thought of it like that." His finger traced the little bird over the inside of my right wrist. "This?"

I sighed. "A hummingbird. They work incredibly hard just to survive, but all the while, they're thriving. Fighting off predators and living life, all while constantly fighting just to stay alive. It's admirable."

Scott's look had softened as he looked at me and it was making me feel funny as our gazes connected in a long, sizzling-hot moment.

"Here you are," Buddy grunted at both of us, breaking the curtain of sexual tension swirling around us.

I frowned. "We didn't order wings and fries." At least I didn't.

"I know, but you're both guzzling back drinks like you're fish. Eat this and give me your keys. Now." Buddy looked like a no-nonsense kind of guy, so I pulled them out and dropped the keys in his hand.

"Thanks, Buddy."

"Anytime, Stevie. This is the last drink for both of you." His gaze bounced from me to Scott, waiting for our acceptance before he left us alone.

"Holy crap, we just got in trouble." I giggled, feeling giddy for some weird reason.

Scott looked around and frowned. "No wonder. We practically shut the place down."

"I guess I'm better company than even I realized."

His green eyes met mine and though I couldn't figure out his expression, I was trapped in his gaze. "Without a doubt."

I rolled my eyes and ignored the pleased feeling that rippled through me at his words. I would not be charmed by Scott. Or flattered. Or any of the other emotions that caused women to go all giggly and flirty. Nope. No way, no how—and definitely not with the boss. "You're not totally boring either, Scott."

"Thanks. I think." His laugh was so damn soothing, like whiskey and honey in a steaming hot mug of tea.

"Out of questions?" We hadn't even gotten to the good stuff yet and he'd barely blushed. Maybe four or five times throughout the night. *Maybe.*

"For tonight, I think I am." His gaze was thoughtful and long, as if he was looking right past me and into some other time in his life. It forced at least a dozen more questions to the surface, all of which I refused to ask because that would get me involved. Too involved than I was ready to be in Tulip just yet.

But I could see that Scott had had too much to drink and everyone but Buddy had already gone home, which meant it was time for the Good Samaritan version of myself to kick in. "All right, Doc, let's get you someplace you can zonk out for a few hours."

He frowned and glanced around the empty bar. "I'm going home."

"Maybe, sure. In a few hours. There's no way either of us will make it out to your place before morning, unless you have an in with local law enforcement to exploit?"

"I could call, but then we'd have a lot of explaining to do, not to mention the risk that Eddy might show up and we'd end up in a hotel room in Alabama together." He shook his head. "No, thanks."

"Well, maybe you have friends you can crash with, but I don't, so thanks for the company and I'll see you in the morning, Scott." I stood from the booth, feeling a little wobblier than I had a few seconds ago. I gripped the table and paused a moment to get my bearings. "Okay. Good night."

The night air was chilly and a gentle breeze swayed, but I had enough booze and spicy wings inside of me to keep the chill at bay until I found a way back to Scott's guest cottage.

"Stevie, wait up?" I turned in the middle of the parking lot and found Scott's big body jogging my way.

"Afraid to walk the tough streets of Tulip alone?"

He let out another of those snort laughs I was slowly growing addicted to. "Something like that. You gonna protect me?"

I shook my head and fell into step beside Scott's much bigger frame. "You're big enough that I imagine few people ever try to be big shots."

"You'd be surprised. When I first left the NFL Combine, plenty of people wanted to take a shot at me. Maybe it's my size or just giving up on what most people see as a dream come true, but plenty of drunk idiots wanted to have a go. They wanted to fight or race me, or even do a quick scrimmage, if you can believe it."

I barked out a laugh at the ridiculousness of man, but I hadn't forgotten the bomb he'd just dropped. "It's Texas, of course I believe people wanted to fight you for quitting the NFL. Why did you?"

He shrugged. "The idea of putting my body through that for the next twenty years, if I'm lucky, was less and less appealing as the days wore on. Then I got my acceptance to a DVM program, and everything became clear."

"DVM?" I was starting to suspect there was more to Scott than a pretty face and a strait-laced attitude.

"Doctor of Veterinary Medicine."

"Impressive," I sang playfully, but the truth was that it *was* impressive. He'd given up on a ton of money to do something he loved. Something that mattered to more than just him, to more than the spreadsheets.

"You think so?"

"I do. Careful, Scott, or I just might start liking you." I smiled up at him, knowing the truth was that I already liked Scott plenty. He was a good boss, a caring doctor, and a nice man. Plus, he was a delicious piece of man candy—what's there *not* to like?

"You already like me." I saw the intent in his eyes the moment the low timber of his voice hit me right in the chest. He took a step forward. "You might not want to, but you do."

He was right, but I was no longer an impulsive little girl. "Maybe I do, but this is a bad idea," I told him, motioning between our bodies that were now much too close for any kind of logical thinking to take place. "A very bad idea."

"Probably." He stepped in closer and his big hand cupped one side of my face, warm and slightly calloused. "But right now, it seems like the best idea I ever had." Then, before I could think better of it or protest in any way, Scott's lips were on mine. They were strong and firm, surprisingly soft for a man his size. And holy hell, the man knew exactly how to use them.

The top one was a little plumper than the bottom, giving me plenty to savor when our lips met, following by tongues and teeth, and then bodies. Right there on the side of the road, I made out with Dr. Scott Henderson like a horny teenager who was already late for curfew. Instead of pulling back, I leaned in breathlessly and deepened the kiss, intensified it like I was a starving woman and he was a tall drink of water, well, because... he was.

A car siren sounded in the distance, pulling us back like two guilty people who'd been caught with their hands in the cookie jar. "What was that?" He looked as bewildered as I felt and I couldn't help but grin.

"I believe that, dear Scotty, was a kiss. A hell of a kiss, at that." That kiss had stolen my breath and rocked me to my core, but I managed what I hoped was a flirty smile.

"No shit," he grunted and pulled me against his side as a truck slowed beside us on the road.

So, the good doctor wasn't as much of a straight arrow as he appeared.

Very interesting.

SCOTT

Three days had passed since the kiss that had rocked my world, and I hadn't been able to stop thinking about it. Or Stevie, damn her. After putting up with more crap than I wanted to deal with from the sheriff, Ty—who did his big brother diligence and gave me plenty of shit for getting caught making out with a girl on the side of the road—gave us a lift home. The ride had been short and tense, and I would have given anything to know what was on her mind.

In fact, when I woke up the next morning after arranging a ride for us to get our cars, she was already gone. Had picked up her car without a word, and when I got back home, she was parked behind the guest cottage. It was Wednesday morning and I'd given her plenty of time to come say something, anything, about 'The Kiss', because that was how I'd been thinking about it. Pretty much nonstop. So far, Stevie had defied the odds and kept whatever she was feeling to herself.

It was a curse and a relief.

A sharp, efficient knock sounded on the door and I sat up, alert. "Come in."

The door opened and Stevie stood there, her mass of black hair tied back into a high ponytail that never stopped moving and her plump pink lips drawing my gaze against the backdrop of her milky skin. She had black stuff on her eyelashes that made them look a mile long, but otherwise, Stevie looked like... Stevie. She wore a lavender t-shirt that hugged her tits and barely brushed the top of her fitted jeans. Really fitted jeans that pulled my eye to the curve of her hip, the dip between her thighs. "There's some kind of emergency in Peak's Ridge. Neglected, possibly abused animals. At least two."

So much for those thoughts. I was on my feet, fast. People in this part of the world treated their animals kindly and often relied on them for their livelihood, but some people fell on hard times, and others—well, others were just assholes and mistreated animals because they could. "All right. Grab a couple emergency rescue kits and meet me at the truck."

She nodded and left my office as quickly and quietly as she'd entered. I grabbed my bag along with a few extra supplies and took a deep breath before I made my way to the front office. "Of course, Mrs. Slattery, I have you booked first thing tomorrow and if this run doesn't take too long, I'll give you a call. Promise." Stevie flashed a professional smile and ended the call before turning and offering me a blander version of the same smile. "The kits are already in your truck and I've rescheduled nearly all of today's appointments."

"Perfect. That means you can come with me." I don't know what possessed me to say that, but Stevie nodded and stood as she finished typing.

"I need five minutes to finish these calls and I'll meet you in the truck." She didn't sound bothered or like she might try to wiggle out of going so I nodded and made my way outside, preparing myself for spending time with her in my truck, which usually seemed huge. Today, as I climbed inside and flipped on the air conditioning, it felt like a box. A tiny, suffocating box.

A few minutes later, she came out carrying a box almost as big as she was. She set it on the ground, giving me a glimpse of her round ass that, as her boss, I shouldn't even notice, while she locked the door. Finally, what felt like hours later, she hopped in the passenger seat and flashed a smile at me.

"Okay, boss man, let's hop to it."

The car was on the move and we drove towards the interstate in silence. In absolute silence, but it wasn't a tense silence, thank goodness. "Don't do anything crazy when we get there and let me do the talking."

Stevie snorted and shook her head. "Really?"

"Yes. These situations can turn bad quickly, Stevie, and I don't want you to get hurt."

She folded her arms and notched her chin up in a sign I recognized as defiance. "I don't want you to get hurt, either. And last I checked, you were a doctor, not a cop."

Confrontation swam in her violet eyes and, as amused as I was, I needed to make myself clear.

"No, but I am a man. A big one, at that." I held up my hands to stop whatever smart ass remark she was about to let out. "That alone usually encourages people, *mostly men*, against starting trouble."

She sank back against the passenger seat and sighed. "Fine. I'll let the big man do the talking, but if I can help, I will."

She wouldn't, but there would be no point telling her that now. "Are you all settled in at the cottage?"

Stevie nodded, her gaze fixed on a point in the road. "Yep. The place is nice and cozy. Far from town, though." I wondered if she would use this as a way to bring up the kiss, but a minute passed and she said nothing else.

"You'll appreciate it once you get more acquainted with the meddlers." Being difficult to get to made it easy to stay out of their crosshairs. Mostly.

Stevie turned to me, a sly smile on her face as we crossed the sign that led to what used to be Carmichael Ranch. "I don't know, Scott, those ladies seem pretty spritely to me. When they want to, I have a feeling they'll find their way to you just fine."

I glared at her and shifted the car into park before killing the engine. "Bite your tongue."

With a comical smack of her lips, Stevie snapped her mouth shut and looked around at Carmichael Ranch. "What the hell is this dump, and how do they have any animals here?"

She wasn't wrong. The main house of the ranch was a

filthy white that likely hadn't been washed in years. The screen door was half-fixed to the hinges and the top wooden stair was missing, making it a hazard. "Probably why we got the call." I jumped from the truck and looked around at the property. The land was in worse condition than the house, somehow, with barely a hint of grass anywhere and hard, brittle dirt as far as the eye could see.

"Scott, look!" Stevie was already headed toward the small cage and the whining creature inside. "You're a pretty boy, aren't you," she cooed and held her hand up to the cage so the chocolate lab puppy could smell her. He whined and Stevie opened the cage.

"Wait!" I put a hand on her wrist and glared at her. "Slowly. This dog might have been abused."

"Clearly." She rolled her eyes and shook off my hold, opening the cage and giving the puppy time to come to her. "You're all right, aren't you, boy? Come on out, I've got some water for you." She produced a bottle and waved it in front of the pup. "You know you want it," she teased before producing a bowl and pouring the water inside, then scooting back.

"I thought you were gonna let me lead."

She laughed. "I will. When it comes to big scary humans who want to fight." Stevie stood and wiped the dirt and grass from her butt, a wide grin on her face. "Oh, look, he's drinking it."

I looked on as the puppy lapped up the water greedily until it was empty, and he turned big brown eyes up at Stevie with a whine. "Now you've done it."

She wasn't paying attention to me, though. Her attention was fully on the dog as she crouched down and poured more water with one hand and gave him a rub with the other as a reason to check the tag. "Hershey. Cute."

It was cute but, dammit, Hershey had been severely neglected and he couldn't be more than six to eight months old. He was malnourished, underweight, and scared of his own shadow. "Let's go see what's in the barn," I barked and started to walk. I could hear Stevie talking to the dog.

"Stay here," she told him and caught up with me at the entrance of the barn. "Holy hell, it smells worse than a barn in here."

My nostrils flared and I steeled myself for what I knew might find. "Stay behind me. Please."

"Fine," she groaned and I felt her breath on my back.

"Dammit." The yearling was a golden-colored filly with a matted blond mane, ribs poking out and legs weak and wobbly. "Son of a bitch," I bit out and slowly approached. "Hey, girl." The horse let out a startled neigh and looked to me with wide, scared eyes. "It's okay. I'm here." I set my bag down and went to the door, coaxing her to me.

"Here." Stevie shoved something soft and moist in my hand. "Use these."

I looked down at the apple slices and frowned. "Where in the hell did you get this?"

She turned and showed the bag flung over one arm. "I have oats, too, but I think the apple will work just fine."

She was right, of course. The filly ate the slices and

begged for more, suddenly no longer afraid of me. It took two full apples, but eventually we got her out of the barn and towards the trailer hitched to my truck. "Let's just get this over with." I couldn't stand to see another living creature suffering, especially so unnecessarily, and the longer we stayed here, the angrier I would become.

"I'll go get Hershey and meet you at the car."

"Wait. Look." The pup was back in the small cage and the bowl was overturned. "Go to the car, Stevie. Now."

"But—" Any words of defiance she'd been about to issue died at the sound of a gun cocking.

"Now, Stevie."

"Fine," she grunted and jogged towards the car. "Come on, girl." She patted her hip and, surprisingly, the horse wobbled after her. Slowly.

"Yeah, Stevie, go now or you'll find buckshot in your pretty little backside. You'd better get yourself gone, too, or I won't hesitate to shoot." The man stepped into the light from the shadows, the shotgun in his hand aimed right at me.

"You don't want to do this, Mr. Carmichael. We just want the animals, but if I have to get the sheriff involved, it *will* include charges of neglect and abuse of an animal. That's a serious crime in this part of the state."

The man grunted and kept his gun trained on me. "These are my animals and you can't just take'em from me, damn you."

"That's where you're wrong. It's my duty as a veterinarian to rescue these animals and get them back to good health." It would take time and resources I didn't have, but I always found a way.

He snorted. "Then you turn around and sell 'em, I'm sure."

"You expect me to give them back to you after you how treated them?" This guy was lower than dirt as far, as I was concerned. "You chose to have these animals and decided not to take care of them. You. Not me or any future owners they might have. *You*."

I knew immediately it was the wrong thing to say when his thick finger slid to the trigger. "Like you would even understand, a fancy vet like you, coming out here to steal my animals and profit off them." He shook his head, growing madder by the moment. "You can't just take'em."

Another gun cocked and I froze, unsure if I should look for the new potential shooter or focus on the one in front of me. "Oh, that's where you're wrong, mister. We have every right to take these animals. The question is, are you gonna make us do this the hard way?"

Stevie? I turned and glared at her, but her gaze was fixed on Mr. Carmichael. "What the hell?"

She nodded toward the dog. "Get Hershey. Goldie is already in the trailer."

"Goldie?"

"Later, Scott. Grab Hershey," she said again and raised the barrel higher, as if readjusting her aim on Mr. Carmichael. "And if you try to shoot at my friend here, I'll make sure you're filled with more than buckshot. Got me?"

He laughed. Tossed his head back and laughed, like

he'd just heard the funniest dirty joke the world had ever heard. "Do you even know how to use that thing, little girl? You sound like a city girl to me."

Stevie looked at the old break-action shotgun she'd found in my truck like it was a new piece of technology. "I'm better with a nine millimeter, but the gist is the same right? Point"—she aimed the gun right at Mr. Carmichael's chest and smiled—"and shoot. Right?"

Carmichael's eyes rounded in fear, over whether she was a novice or crazy enough to shoot him, I didn't know. But I knew his fear was genuine. "Crazy woman," he grumbled and lowered his weapon. "Take the damn things, then."

"How old is the pup?"

"Don't know," he snapped. "Found him on the side of the road about six months ago, was a little scrap of nothing then. Cold and wet, until I took him in and took care of him."

Stevie snorted. "Some job you did. He probably would've been better off on his own." She shook her head as I walked towards her with Hershey in my arms, licking my face. "If I hear you have animals out here again, I'm coming back and sticking you in that damn cage, got it?"

Carmichael nodded and grumbled something under his breath before turning away and slipping inside the house, animals already forgotten once again.

Once we had Hershey loaded up and Goldie comfortable in the trailer, we got the hell off the ranch, just in case Carmichael changed his mind. "Are you out of your mind? What in the hell were you thinking?"

Stevie turned to me, a frown on her face. "I'm not out of my mind. In this situation, I was the big strong man rescuing you. Deal with it."

"Are you for real right now?" I couldn't believe this stubborn woman. "You escalated the situation."

"Seems to me I'm the one who settled it. If I waited in the car like you wanted, you two would still be out there dick measuring."

"It was reckless."

"No, it wasn't. I know my way around quite a few guns, thank you very much. This is Texas, after all. Right?"

She had a point. Ty and I had been around guns since we were boys. You needed them when you drove country roads and spent time in the wild. "It was still reckless," I said, instead of any of that.

"It's done," she barked back, folding her arms and looking out the passenger window, effectively dismissing me.

It was done, dammit, but it still didn't sit right with me, a woman coming to my rescue. No matter how hot she'd looked holding that shotgun, and no matter how old-fashioned and sexist it sounded, it was how I felt.

But there was something else. The more I learned about Stevie, the more I wanted to know about her.

STEVIE

*B*ig Mama's Diner had the most eclectic menu of any small-town diner I'd ever seen, but nothing beats a big fat juicy burger. Even still, I took my time going through the menu to make sure the crazy old proprietress hadn't added anything new since I got to town.

"Stevie. Fancy seeing you again." Ginger flashed a wide smile when she spotted me as she came out the kitchen with two hot plates on one arm and a carafe of juice in another. "I'll be with you in a sec."

"No worries," I told her and turned back to the menu, even though I already knew what I wanted and I was pretty sure Scott would appreciate a healthier version of whatever I ordered. The man forgot about lunch more often than not, skipping it completely when the office wasn't busy, which was almost never since he was the only animal doctor in town.

"All right, what can I get ya?"

That was easy enough. "A bacon burger with extra ketchup and no cheese. A turkey burger with everything but cheese. Two orders of fries and a chocolate milkshake."

Ginger's chestnut brows rose. "Someone's hungry. Or is this for the big man?" The quirk of her lips told me she had something else on her mind and I started to feel antsy, the way I usually felt when it was time to move on.

"Lunch for me and for Dr. Henderson." It was better to remain formal in public since this town had a hankering for matchmaking. Who knew? "That's all."

"Hmm," she said vaguely, ripping the order sheet from the pad and sliding it to the cook. "I heard you were a pretty big badass with a shotgun." This time, her smile bloomed big and bright as she shook her head. "Never would've guessed it about you, though."

I frowned as two thoughts competed for authority. The first was wondering how in the hell she'd heard about that, since Scott didn't seem like the gossiping sort. The second was a bit more personal. "That's what the old man said. Why is it so hard to believe?"

Ginger shrugged, unmoved by my emotions. "You've got the whole city-girl thing going on, kind of like Nina only more... citified, I guess." She shrugged again. "I'm guessing all you need is a little time." She smirked and shook her head, like she was in on some joke the rest of us weren't. "But if you wouldn't mind sitting down for an interview for the paper, that would be great."

Luckily, Big Mama chose that moment to make her appearance with a broad smile and her newly-designed shirts with Big Mama's splashed across the front. "Stevie, I thought I heard you out here, girl. I heard you handled that old Carmichael coot but good." She smacked the counter and laughed. "Lunch is on me today, because you've got spunk. And balls." She held up a closed fist and I assumed she wanted a bump, so I gave it to her. "All right! If you need anything, don't hesitate to ask."

I didn't know what I was supposed to need, but I nodded and returned the money to my back pocket. "Thanks, but it's not necessary. I just wanted to get out of there, and the gun seemed like the easiest way to make that happen." And to make sure he thought twice about firing at Scott.

Big Mama huffed her displeasure at the way I downplayed events—in just ten days, I'd learned just how much the good folks to Tulip loved drama and gossip. Any kind would do, and today, I guessed, it was my turn.

The bell above the door sounded and Eddy walked in with Helen and Betty behind her. The three women didn't look like they were natural friends but, according to Scott, thanks to the Hometown Heroes calendar, matchmaking and meddling had brought them all much closer. I turned away before Eddy could spot me. but it was too late. Not to mention the fact that the diner was small enough that there was no place to hide.

"Three specials please, Ginger, and if you can rush it, we're off to do manicures at the senior home!"

Senior home? I kept my thoughts to myself, grateful the topic of conversation had changed. Ginger nodded and jotted down the order before disappearing into the kitchen. Suddenly, a pair of strong but bony arms wrapped around me and squeezed tight. "Stevie, Scotty told me what you did for him, and though he didn't seem too happy about your heroics, I am genuinely grateful to you for saving his life. Anything you need, don't hesitate to ask. Please."

Big Mama must have seen the discomfort in my eyes because she laughed. "Eddy, let the poor girl breathe."

"Sorry." She pulled back. "It's just… my Scotty."

"I was just doing my job, Eddy. That guy was a jerk and he mistreated his animals." Four sets of eyes were on me and I started to back away until a big wide wall stopped my progress.

"That's my line, isn't it?" It was a deep voice I vaguely recognized but only once I turned did I realize it was Ty, Scott's older brother. And Sheriff of Tulip, the one who'd caught us kissing on the side of the road.

"Sheriff."

"Stevie," he returned, trying hard not to laugh. "Seems like you saved his life, if the rumors are true."

I shook my head, doing a sneaky look around to see where the hell Ginger was with my order. "No, I saved the most adorable puppy in the world and a scared filly. Scott was never really in any danger." Mostly.

"So modest, too," Big Mama added with a smile as she boxed up two slices of pie I didn't order and placed it in my bag, which was growing bigger by the minute. "I like you, Stevie."

"Uh, thanks." I grabbed the bag and made my escape before anyone could ask any more questions.

SCOTT

$\mathcal{I}$ stood in front of the reception desk for several long moments, watching Stevie work. She bit down on her bottom lip when she was deep in concentration, turning it an even brighter shade of pink. She continued working as if unaware of my presence, but I knew that couldn't be true.

"Eddy's invited you to dinner tomorrow night."

My words didn't startle her, which meant she'd known I was there the entire time. Her gaze moved slowly, but eventually, those violet orbs made their way to mine. I couldn't read the emotion in them until a small crinkle formed between her ebony brows.

"Not that I'm in the habit of turning down a free, home-cooked meal, but why?"

She was a suspicious little thing, and that intrigued me further. Stevie was a woman full of secrets. For now, though, I was on a mission.

"For saving my life, just in case you haven't heard."

Because I'd heard about it at least a thousand times since I'd made the foolish, rookie mistake of confiding in Eddy. One stupid little rant about Stevie going off half-cocked at the Carmichael Ranch and my fate had been sealed. My own frustration had gotten the better of me and now I, and Stevie, would have to pay the price.

"When will this end?" she groaned, banging her fore-head against the wrist rest in front of her keyboard. After a few moments of self-abuse, she looked at me and sighed. "Tell your grandmother I'd love to come for dinner. I'll even bring whiskey."

"Make it Irish, and she won't kick you out before dinner begins." I smiled playfully at her so she knew I was joking.

"Good to know." Her lips twitched in amusement, and I would have given anything to know what she was think-ing. "How's Hershey?"

Guess I'd find out later. "Good. He's settling in at home and I'm hoping once he's properly socialized, I can bring him to work with me."

She smiled. "Like a therapy dog, but for other animals?"

"Something like that, yeah." It sounded better than being too busy to take care of another living creature. "He eats like a horse, though, so I might have to rethink this whole having-a-pet thing."

Stevie laughed, and the sound was rich and deep. "He's adorable so you could do worse, as far as pets go."

"He is pretty damn adorable, and he's got so much energy." I'd forgotten just how energetic puppies could be until a session of fetch dragged on into the second hour. "He's been enjoying my morning run, though, so when I go home to feed him, he hasn't destroyed my place."

She laughed again, and the smile even made it to her eyes. "Did you manage to grab yourself something to eat while you were there?"

I felt the heat flame my cheeks as I shook my head, feeling embarrassed that instead of my assistant, she'd taken on the role of caretaker, as well. "No. I wasn't even thinking about me."

Her lips twitched. "Admirable in a doctor, but ridiculous in a grown man." Stevie pushed a stray lock of hair from her face and flashed another of those amused grins. "There's a burger on your desk and thirty minutes until the next appointment arrives." She nodded back toward the office and waited for me to go.

"Trying to get rid of me?"

"No, but if you stand here any longer, someone will stop in to ask you a question and next thing you know, lunch will be over and you'll be elbow-deep in a pregnant Dachshund."

She was right about the first part, and I wasn't even touching the second part of that statement. "Thanks, Stevie. You're the best." I made my way down the hall and headed towards the office, her laughter ringing behind me.

"That's what I've been trying to tell you, Doc!"

Her words stayed with me as I entered the quiet office and attacked the burger and fries that were waiting for me from Big Mama. Despite the tattoos and wild hair, and her distinctly unprofessional appearance, Stevie was the best damn assistant I ever had. And the most tempting, dammit. Hiring her was supposed to stop this desire, but if Eddy's matchmaking and Stevie's tattoos couldn't stop it, could anything?

I wasn't sure, but I was equally unsure if it mattered, in the end. Would all the strikes against her matter against the heat and chemistry between us?

STEVIE

"So, honey, you got a boyfriend?" Eddy's question wasn't all that surprising, considering she'd been asking questions like that since I'd showed up for dinner an hour ago. It didn't seem to matter that Scott and Ty were both seated at the table, or that Janey had shown up for some reason fifteen minutes ago. All that mattered was my love life. Past and present.

"No, Eddy, I don't. And I'm not looking." I figured it was best to cut her off before she got a good head of steam going, but the old woman was tough as hell.

"Well, why not?" She frowned, genuinely confused. "Are you interested in getting a girlfriend? Because if you are, I ain't judging. I just have to... readjust my expectations." Her sly smile reminded me that this woman was clever. Too clever for her own good, and mine.

"I'm not interested in dating right now, Eddy. I have a lot of other things on my mind." Particularly, how long I would be employed by Scott. After that kiss, I wasn't sure how long he'd be willing to keep me on, so I was keeping my head down and doing my job to the best of my ability. If he fired me, the reasons would be strictly personal.

"Such as?" Eddy arched a brow and leaned forward, resting her chin in her hand.

"Such as my job, which I just got and there's no guarantee will be there tomorrow or the next day." I sent an apologetic look at Scott, who looked back at me like a deer caught in headlights. "Sorry, but it's true. He doesn't want or need an assistant, and I refuse to start anything with the future being so uncertain." There. That sounded well thought-out and mature, surely Eddy could respect that.

"Oh, that's bull, and you and I both know it. Life is filled with uncertainty—you might as well enjoy every moment while you can." She flashed a smile, so proud of her argument which, I could admit, was a winning one.

"Maybe so, but if my stay here is temporary, then I don't want to get attached."

"Some people come to Tulip for a visit and end up staying for love," Janey put in with a mischievous smile.

"Yeah?" My question was smug, because this sounded like one of those things people said to win an argument but when pressed, couldn't come up with one example. "Who?"

Ty and Scott both groaned at the question, the first sign of my misstep. A satisfied grin split Janey's face in half. "Tulip. She came here to see about starting over and fell in love with a farmer. Together, they built a flower empire and this awesome little town."

It was a nice story, one I'd read about online before coming here and had heard at least half a dozen times since I arrived. But it still didn't change the facts of my life. "Sounds like you might have more luck hooking Janey up with some stranger passing through town, Eddy." Everyone laughed and the tension that had been ratcheting up in the room disappeared.

Janey sucked in a breath and narrowed her gaze at me. "Thanks for that."

"You're welcome." To stop any more questions or answers, I shoved a slice of juicy lamb in my mouth with a smile and focused on my plate. The food was delicious, lamb and roasted vegetables with the most delicious garlic mashed potatoes I had ever eaten. "This food is amazing, Eddy. Almost worth the interrogation."

"Only almost?" She huffed her disbelief at my words. "Guess I'll have to have you around again to remove that *almost*."

I laughed around a comically large mouthful of potatoes. "I'm willing to try if you are."

Eddy glared for a long moment and then erupted in a loud, raucous laugh. "I like you, Stevie."

"Thanks, Eddy. You're a little crazy, but I like you, too. And your roast lamb."

Her grin lit up. "You sure you don't want a boyfriend? My grandsons are two of the handsomest bachelors in town." Eddy did her best game show hostess impersonation as she waved her hands in the direction of Ty, then Scott, just in case they weren't sufficiently on display. "Aren't they, Janey?"

Her cheeks turned pink, and I thought maybe she did have a crush on one of the Henderson brothers. "Uh, sure. They're all right, I mean. You know."

Very interesting. "They are very handsome, Eddy, but I'm sure you know it takes more than that to have a relationship. Unless you're trying to pimp these hotties out?" Both men erupted in simultaneous fits of coughing, with Ty taking time to shoot a glare in my direction while he choked. "Not a bad side hustle for the calendar, Janey."

Eddy was howling with laughter as she stood. "On that note, dessert is optional."

I stood, shoving the last carrot in my mouth and following behind Eddy. "I'll help with the dishes and take my dessert to go, if you don't mind."

"Not at all, honey. It'll be nice to have someone to chat with while I clean up."

I grabbed the plate from her hand. "*I'll* wash and you can dry. Since you did all the cooking."

Eddy wanted to argue, I could see in her eyes and the tense set of her shoulders, but she surprised me and gave in easily. "Fine. Thank you, Stevie."

I smiled. "Thanks for dinner." I couldn't remember the last time I had a home-cooked meal.

"Anytime. Usually, I invite more people, but I didn't want to embarrass you by questioning you in front of other folks."

I snorted a laugh. "But you thought it would be fine in front of my boss? You really are a crazy ol' lady, Eddy. You know that?"

She put one finger to her lips. "You've figured me out, but don't go spreading that around."

I didn't think it was as much of a secret as Eddy thought, but I locked my lips and tossed away the key just to ease her mind. "Your secret is safe with me."

"Perfect. Now tell me what you really think of my—" She held up a finger as a phone rang in the distance, with a classical song that played. And played. "That's me. Be right back." Eddy took off at a pace far too fast for her age and I shook my head with a smile, hoping I'd have as much energy when I was her age.

Dinner had gone well, at least as far as I was concerned. It was a little strange to be invited to the boss's family home for dinner, but I was learning very quickly that Tulip was unlike any other place I'd ever lived. My thoughts went in a variety of directions while I cleaned the dishes, steadfastly avoiding all six-foot-tall, green-eyed distractions.

"Need some help?" I knew that voice well. Better than anyone else's in town, and I froze at his question.

"I've got it, thanks." My gaze remained on the soapy water until Scott was gone. Or until I *thought* he was.

"You can't do all the dishes by yourself."

"Why not? I'm the one who offered."

Scott took the plate from my hand and picked up the towel. "And now, I'm offering to replace my grandma."

"Whether I want you to or not?" I tried to take a step back but there was no place to go, unless I wanted to jump into the oversized roasting pan to hide. Which I kind of did.

"Didn't realize my help was such a burden," he said, a smile curling his lips despite the fake outrage in his tone.

"Did I say that? Because I'm pretty sure I said, 'I've got it,' as in I don't *need* any help. I'm not a doctor, but I have done dishes before. Have you?"

One blonde brow arched in surprise. "Does Eddy seem like the kind of woman who'd let me reach this age without doing dishes?"

"Maybe not, but that was ages ago, when you were a kid." Why was this so much fun and why on earth was my heart racing like I was doing CrossFit? I was exhilarated, I realized. Verbally sparring with Scott was fun and exciting. Thrilling, even. Which spelled trouble.

He plucked another plate from my hand. "Like riding a bike. See?" Scott made a big show out of drying the plate and putting it away. "Hit me with another."

"Don't tempt me," I grumbled and looked up at him, which was a big mistake because his deep green gaze ensnared my own and I was transfixed. Unable to move, because his gaze held me so steadily. The moment was charged, as electricity arced back and forth between us. This was one of those *moments* people always talked about, but that I had dismissed because I'd never experienced them before. But this was a whole new beast that I didn't understand, and I wasn't sure if I wanted to.

"You wouldn't dare." His grin teased and I felt it all the way down to my knees, leaning against the sink to keep myself upright.

"I might," I told him with a cheeky grin that slowly faded as the look in his eyes darkened with heat that could have been desire. He looked like he wanted to kiss me, which was bad news because in that moment I was pretty sure I would let him. Then, the sound of a camera drew my attention.

Scott groaned. "Janey, what the hell?"

"What?" The question came out far too innocent, and I'd only known Janey for a few days. "You're a Hometown Hero and I don't have nearly enough pictures of you."

"Janey," he growled.

"Ugh, fine." She rolled her eyes at Scott, treating him more like an annoying sibling than a man she was crushing on, which was even more interesting than his growl. "Damn, that's a good shot, though. Really hot, too." She looked up and winked at me before she waved and left us alone. Again.

"What was that about?"

He shook his head. "You don't want to know. Believe me."

"Now I feel like I need to know, and since we have all the pots and pans to wash, get to talking, Scotty."

He glared at my use of his dreaded nickname, but when I handed him another dish, he dried it. And got to talking, the almost-kiss nothing but a memory.

SCOTT

I wasn't normally much of a drinker. Sure, I enjoyed a few beers during trivia night at Black Thumb or just hanging out with the guys, but I wasn't one to sit around and drink by myself. Until today, apparently. After a dinner that felt far too long for my liking, I made my way home and realized I had nothing to do.

Thanks to Stevie, there was no longer after-hours work required. There were no invoices to send off, no files to catch up on, and no bills to pay, because she took care of it. *All* of it. Having Stevie in the office made my job and my life easier, which I appreciated. But her words from dinner kept playing in my head. *He doesn't want or need an assistant.* Did she still really believe that?

I guess I hadn't done much to make her feel welcome after officially hiring her. *Except kissing the hell out of her on the side of the road and almost kissing her in my grandma's kitchen.* I especially couldn't stop thinking about that moment in Eddy's kitchen. That *almost* moment, where I'd been thinking about kissing her and she was seriously considering letting me. Stevie was too tough, too independent to ever admit it, but those violet eyes didn't lie. Even now, I regretted that I hadn't leaned in and brushed my lips against hers to see if they were as soft and plump as I remembered.

But I couldn't. Not because I didn't want to, because every passing day made me want to kiss her more and more, but it was all wrong. The timing was wrong. The woman was wrong. Everything was just... wrong. If I started anything with Stevie, she and Eddy might get the wrong idea, and I was in no place to enter into a romantic relationship right now. Something casual and fun? Absolutely. But my clinic was still fairly new, and I needed to build up my business and my reputation with the farmers and ranchers in the area who hadn't known me since I was knee-high to a grasshopper. The mortgage on the office and the property, which I hoped to turn into a rescue or sanctuary in the future, was in its infancy, and all of that was my priority at the moment, not a woman. Not even Stevie.

And even if I was in the market for a relationship, it couldn't be with an employee. No matter how enticing she was. No matter how well she filled out a pair of jeans.

Thankfully, Hershey chose that moment to scratch at the back door, our agreed-upon signal when he needed a visit to the tree out back. "I'm comin', boy." He was just the distraction I needed before my thoughts and my drinking grew out of control. Instead, I focused on the unusually warm night, the clear midnight-blue sky, and the warm air that rustled the trees. It was a beautiful night and I was drinking.

Alone.

"Hershey boy, come on!" I let out a low whistle and looked around at his favorite spots, starting with the big oak behind the house. "Where are you, Hershey?" I whistled again and there was nothing, no sounds of his puppy panting or whining, no overturned flowerpots or any other indication of a boisterous puppy. About halfway between my house and the guest cottage, I heard feminine giggling. "Hershey?"

The dog was in an enviable position on Stevie's lap with his belly exposed as a soft hand gave him all the rubs he could handle. The puppy was in heaven and I couldn't say I blamed him one bit. "You're just a little slut for the belly rubs, aren't you, boy?"

"Pretty sure you can't call a puppy a slut. Can you?"

The sound of my voice startled Stevie, but only for a moment. She recovered quickly and sent a shy smile my way. "He doesn't care what I call him, as long as the rubs don't stop. Isn't that right, Hersh?"

The pup barked and turned so he could put his front paws on her shoulders, almost like he was giving her a hug. And then he did exactly what I'd wanted to do earlier —kiss the hell out of her lush pink mouth. "I guess you made an impression."

She laughed and wrapped her arms around Hershey's little body that appeared much bigger beside her before she stood and wiped away the dirt and grass stuck to her. "The way to a man's heart is apparently belly rubs."

I barely registered her words—the sight of Stevie in sexy, lightweight cotton shorts that showed off her smooth legs, and another tattoo, was about all my brain had the capacity to focus on. The lavender shorts and tank looked like pajamas, which only made me want to peek even closer, to see if the dark outline of her nipples was pink or brown. The tank top was just short enough to reveal an inch-wide swath of pale skin and belly button at her waist, and everything fitted so perfectly I could see every dip and curve of her body. And, just like that, all my good intentions flew out the window.

I wanted Stevie. Bad.

"This has been scintillating conversation, Scott. Really." She patted my shoulder and moved to walk around me, but I grabbed her wrist and pulled her flush against me. "Uh, what are you doing?"

"Something really stupid that I guarantee we'll both enjoy." My mouth crashed down on hers in a storm of lips and tongue and teeth. I was like a man possessed, tasting every inch of her mouth until my blood boiled and my whole body was tense. Hard. Throbbing.

I thought Stevie might put up a token protest, if for no other reason than to maintain her tough-girl image; instead, she shocked me by melting into my embrace and wrapping her arms around my neck. When her tentative fingertips brushed the hair at the nape of my neck, a shiver shot through me. The kiss went on, right there on the small patch of grass outside of Stevie's cottage with nothing but the moon and Hershey watching us.

My hands roamed, touching every bit of her they'd longed to since she'd landed in my office. Uninvited. Now, though, that seemed so long ago and I couldn't seem to remember why I had objected so much, especially with the soft dip of her hips nestled perfectly in the cup of my hand and the way her ass was made for squeezing. Up and down her petite frame, my hands glided and explored until it was all memorized.

Stevie pulled back with a gasp, wide eyed and panting. "What… what was that?"

My heart thundered as rapidly as the pulse at the base of her neck, which I found fascinating. A wide smile lit my face, and Stevie's lit in response. "That was a damn fine start, Stevie." And because I couldn't help myself, my lips found hers again, this time plundering until her hands tightened around my shoulder and her soft breasts were smashed up against my chest, the sound of her heartbeat merged with my own.

Then, Stevie was airborne, flying through the air until we were face to face and her legs wrapped around my waist. "Much better," she said on a breathless smile and then dove in for another kiss that was hotter and more out of control than the previous two.

My feet began to move toward the open entry to the cottage, my body already decided on the outcome. I hesitated at the door, giving Stevie a chance to tell me to get lost in her own special way and when her fingers wrapped around my hair, I had my answer. With her petite frame in my arms, I was no longer able to control my need for her. As soon as the door slammed shut behind us, she slid down my body and I removed her clothes and stared. "Shit, Stevie."

She grinned at me even as a pleased blush stained her cheeks, and wiggled her hips. "Thanks, but I think one of us is now a tad overdressed." Her gaze slid over my body as if she was already imagining me naked, and that heated look in her violet eyes turned my blood to fire and my cock to stone. Stevie closed the small space between us and let her hands slide up my chest and over my shoulders before they went down my back, squeezing my ass.

"Stevie," I groaned but she only laughed as her hands made quick work of my clothes, undressing me until I stood before her in nothing but a pair of boxer briefs.

"I approve, Scotty. I definitely approve." The teasing smile on her lush lips, or maybe her cheeky use of my nickname, was what finally sapped the last of my willpower because I had her in my arms, my mouth searing her flesh with fiery kisses and soothing them with my tongue. "Yes!"

That was exactly the level of enthusiasm I was hoping for and I kept it up, letting the sounds of her pleasure guide me as I lowered us to the bed and devoured her mouth. It was like someone cranked up the heat in the cottage—suddenly, we were slicked with sweat, limbs moving frantically like it was some kind of race. "Slow down."

Stevie froze and looked at me, licking her lips slowly. "Why, when fast is so much more fun?"

I couldn't deny that, but still, if she kept moving her hands the way she was and grinding against me, this would be over before it even got going. My hands went to her hips to slow them and she let out a sexy little pout that only made mharder, made me want her more.

"I agree," I told her and flipped us so I was on top of her, my weight pressing her into the mattress, my cock nestled in the cradle of her thighs. "Yeah, that's better."

"Much," she groaned and wiggled her hips, bucking up into me. "Feel free to get moving."

My lips twitched in amusement, but there was nothing funny about the way she tempted me beyond all reason. I teased her for several long minutes, kissing her neck while my fingers tested the sweet damp heat between her thighs. Stevie was ready, and knowing she wanted this so badly made me want her even more. "I will." Eventually.

Watching Stevie squirm with unsated desire was like watching live erotica, the way her tits jiggled every time she tried to urge me to move, the way her scent wafted between us as I stroked her. "Scott, please."

The sound of that particular word coming from her mouth was what finally pushed me over the edge. I shifted back, cock in my hand, and stroked it while I looked down at her and inhaled the scent of her arousal. "Please?"

She nodded. "Please. *Now*, please." Stevie flashed a cheeky grin and reached between us to wrap her fingers around my cock. "Please." I let her guide me in, because I was powerless to do anything else with her hand on me, sliding me slowly into her body.

"Oh, fuck!"

"Yeah, that's better," she growled and arched into me, digging her heels into my ass.

I smiled—Stevie was a talker, but very few words were said after that point. We came together in a firestorm of grunts and moans, arms and legs, bodies smacking together as we chased down pleasure, hard and fast, until we were both sated and happy, maybe a little delirious from our encounter. "Wow." I looked over at Stevie, surprise and maybe even a little bit of wonder on my face. "That was... incredible."

"No kidding," she agreed with a breathless laugh. "It was definitely a 'wow.'"

She was wrong. It wasn't just a 'wow' kind of thing, it was more than that. So much more than that. It wasn't just good or erotic or hot as fuck, it was something else, something I couldn't quite name, almost as if the word or emotion was just out of my reach. It was a scary feeling and I didn't want to ruin the moment, the afterglow, by thinking about it.

So I turned to Stevie with a wicked smile on my face. "Maybe we ought to do that again, just to make sure it was wow."

Stevie looked at me seriously and then a husky laugh erupted from her, making her tits jiggle beautifully. I leaned forward and pulled a hard, raspberry-tipped nipple into my mouth, getting her revved up for round two.

aking up the morning after you've had the most reinvigorating sex of your life feels like waking up... reborn. I know how it sounds, all sappy and cheesy and over-the-top poetic, but it was true. Maybe it was because I hadn't *had* sex in more than a year, maybe longer, but after a while you kind of just stop counting. Or, maybe, it was the man. Scott was an incredible lover, the kind who went out of his way to make sure you were completely satisfied before he looked after his own pleasure. And last night, he'd done a damn good job of looking after my pleasure, so I returned the favor. Happily.

But it was time to push all thoughts of sexy time out of my mind and get to work, so I unfolded my sore muscles from the rumpled bed sheets and took a quick shower, as hot as I could stand it until the scent of Scott was no longer on my skin. Then I got dressed, put on a cup of coffee courtesy of the one-cup pot that was in the cottage when I arrived, and was out the door with fifteen minutes to spare.

The office was quiet, which meant Scott hadn't left my bed to get into the office early. That meant he'd *just* left. And that was just fine with me. I wasn't well-versed in morning-after etiquette, and I'd rather not embarrass myself in front of him. Or anyone. That made things easier for me, actually, because now I didn't have to worry about what last night meant. Was it the start of something, or just a one-time thing? The answer was clear.

And that clarity put a pep in my step—or maybe it was the four orgasms from last night. Either way, I moved about the office with purpose, full of energy and efficiency. When the first appointments began to arrive, I slapped on a professional smile and played the role of dutiful assistant to a tee.

"All set, Elka?" The strawberry blonde was about twenty months pregnant, with a small brown bunny tucked under her arm.

"Yep. Scott says he's all clear. Just a small case of getting more than he bargained for, when he went snooping in the woods behind the house." Her laugh was pretty and feminine, just like the woman—a stark contrast to the tall, dark, and brooding man waiting for her by the door.

"Awesome. I'll put the bill in the mail. Enjoy the rest of your day." She gave me a short wave and waddled out of the office to greet her man with a kiss hot enough to make me blush, even through the thick window.

Lunch came and went, but both Scott and I were too

swamped to even stop for food, so when Eddy showed up with two greasy bags from Big Mama's, I was happy to see her. Mostly. "Hello, Stevie. How are you today, dear?"

I smiled and looked up at her as if nothing at all was wrong, because nothing *was* wrong, despite the gorgeous blonde standing beside her with a chihuahua pup in her arms. Actually, it was in a small leather cage. Or maybe it was a purse. "I'm good, Eddy. What brings you by?"

"Do you know Clara? This is Clara Cartwright, and she just moved to Langley from Dallas." Eddy smiled proudly, as if she or Clara had built one of those cities instead of just hailed from one or both of them.

"Nice to meet you, Clara. I assume you're here for this guy?" The puppy was friendly enough, sniffing me and licking my finger.

"Yes. Ralphie is about three months and it's time for his next round of shots."

"Perfect. Fill this out, and I'll get you back as soon as I can." I handed her the paperwork and Clara took the clipboard before teetering her way to the chairs in three-inch heels. I turned to Eddy with a grin. "Please tell me one of those bags is for me?"

She set both bags in front of me and I hurried and pulled them behind the desk to avoid greasy paperwork. "Yeah, one's for you. Big Mama said you didn't come in today."

"Thanks, Eddy."

"Thanks for what?" Scott, of course, chose that moment to make his presence known, and his grandmother's face lit up.

"Eddy brought us lunch." I handed one of the bags to him without looking and peeked inside my own to see what I would be eating when and if this place cleared out for more than five minutes.

"Thanks." He grinned and leaned forward, pressing a kiss to the older woman's cheek. "You're the best, you know that?"

"Of course, I do," she cooed like a flirty teenager. "Do you know Clara?" Eddy went through her whole spiel again, but when she added extra details, I was on to the old lady. "Clara is an attorney over in Langley. Just joined that big firm."

Scott's blond brows dipped into a confused vee. "Okay. Nice to meet you, Carla."

My lips twitched behind the computer screen as Eddy let out a disappointed groan. "It's Clara, Scotty."

"Clara Cartwright," I added with a cheeky grin. "And her puppy Ralphie."

Clara chose that moment to join the conversation, a broad smile on her face and her ultra-tanned cleavage pushed out on full display. "That's right, I'm Clara, and this is Ralphie. Nice to meet you, Dr. Henderson." She purred the words, like an *actual* purr, and I wondered if I'd missed that day at school because I couldn't do that. She put one delicate hand in his, iridescent pink nails shimmering under the fluorescent lights.

"You, too." He turned to me for a rescue but not only was I not a particularly jealous person—unless we're talking about Elon Musk or Jeff Bezos—I was also having too much fun watching it all play out. Clara was gorgeous and thin with giant boobs, well put-together and she seemed nice. Oh, she was also a lawyer, which meant she was beautiful *and* accomplished. If Scott was interested in Eddy's newest attempt at matchmaking, he could do worse.

"They're here for Ralphie's round two immunizations."

Relief flashed briefly and he clutched his lunch bag even tighter. "Uh, okay. Do we have room in the schedule?"

"Yep! I'll get her set up in exam room three while you take notes on the last appointment," I told him, glancing down at said sandwich bag. "Fifteen minutes?"

He nodded and I hopped up like my backside was on fire, rushing away from the suddenly awkward foursome —five, if you included Ralphie—to prep the exam room. I took my time and when I returned to take Clara and Ralphie to the room, Eddy was still there.

"She's nice, isn't she?"

"She is. Pretty, too," I added just to let the old girl know I was on to her schemes.

"Very. Accomplished also. A lawyer." Eddy did a terrible job of hiding the smirk on her face.

"At that new firm over in Langley," I added with a short laugh. "I know what you're up to, old woman, and I don't like it." I pointed at her, noticing that unlike Clara's, my nails were short and jagged—desperately in need of a manicure. I was about a lifetime overdue.

She blinked and a small laugh escaped. "I don't know what you mean." To her credit, she didn't even try to look innocent. Yet.

"You'll have to work a lot harder at being believable, Eddy. You know what you're doing and so do I."

The crafty old bird notched her chin in the air and sniffed. "You'll have to be more specific, Stevie."

She wanted specific? Okay. "If Scott is interested in Clara, that's his business. I have no claims on him, despite all of your meddling."

"You could have claims, if you'd stop acting so damn independent. Now, don't get me wrong, a woman needs to be able to take care of herself without a man, but you act like you don't need anyone—and a man needs to feel needed."

I let her words sink in for a long moment and nodded, because she was right. More than one relationship had ended because I wasn't needy or clingy enough, and usually I watched them go with a relieved smile. "If that's the case, I hope he and Clara are very happy together."

She let out an annoyed sigh and smacked her hand on the closest flat surface. "Dammit, Stevie."

I held up a finger to stop her explanation and grabbed the ringing phone with a smile. "Henderson Animal Clinic, how may I help you?" I flashed the toothiest grin I could in her direction and Eddy glared.

"You'll regret this," she mouthed to me and left with a harrumph.

I smiled and spent the next hour and a half answering phone calls and shuffling patients in and out of the lobby and exam room. The rest of the afternoon flew by so fast I didn't have the time or the energy to think about anything more important than what I would have for dinner tonight.

Not Scott.

Not Scott *and* Clara together.

Not me and Scott. Naked. Together.

Nope, all I thought about was an ice-cold beer and a big plate of Buddy's beef and black bean nachos.

SCOTT

"*W*hat's with the frown?" Ty set down a pitcher of dark beer and took the seat across from me, his ever-present stoic expression firmly in place.

I shrugged, feeling out of sorts as I scanned the after-work crowd at Black Thumb, watching single men and women circle each other while couples canoodled near the digital jukebox, danced too close on the tiny dance floor, or made out in the dark corners surrounding the pool tables in back. "I don't know. Today has been weird."

Ty let out a laugh, waving over Derek and Antonio as they entered. "This is Tulip, every damn day is weird."

He was right about that. This little town could best be described as quirky, and something odd *was* always happening, but since the Hometown Heroes calendar became a town-wide thing, the weirdness factor had only increased. "I know that, but Eddy came in today and she brought in this woman. Clara."

"Was she hot?" Ty asked just as Derek and Antonio arrived at the table with another pitcher of beer, wearing the smiles of the well loved and satisfied man.

"Was who hot?" Antonio's dark brows dipped into a suspicious vee.

"Clara," Ty answered with too much glee. "The woman Eddy brought into his clinic today."

"Woman?" Now it was Derek's turn to look confused. "What happened to Stevie? Maxine said that's who they had their eye on for you."

Though it was nice to hear confirmation that I wasn't going crazy, that part didn't make sense. "That's what I was thinking, too—I mean, Eddy brought her here and hired her without my knowledge, so what's with Clara?" Women were already confusing, and trying to figure out the logic of a group of meddling middle-aged match-makers was impossible.

"Maybe they realized Stevie isn't your type." Derek's lips quirked and I knew he was thinking about Maxine, so different from him but, somehow, he'd managed to make her fall for him.

"She isn't," I barked a tad too loud. "But that's not the point. Clara was handsy as hell. I had to keep her yapping dog between us as a barrier to prevent her from shoving my face into her cleavage."

Ty barked out a laugh. "Sounds horrible. A gorgeous woman is throwing herself at you." He rolled his eyes. "Give me a break."

"Give your brother a break," Antonio insisted. "He's

attracted to a woman he's convinced is all wrong from him and worse, the whole town is in on it."

"The whole town?" I'd assumed Eddy and her crew were in on it, but the whole damn town?

Ty nodded. "Guess you didn't see the Hometown Heroes Facebook page today?" With the giddiness of a teenage girl meeting her favorite pop star for the first time, Ty pulled out his phone, swiped a few times, and turned the screen so I could see it. "Take it."

I did, and the image staring back at me was… electric. Even the static capture that should have come across as flat and lifeless was hot. Fiery and filled with sexual tension. Looking at the photo of me and Stevie in Eddy's kitchen, it wasn't hard to predict what had happened later that night. "Janey."

Derek and Antonio both laughed, because they'd both been caught in similar situations by the pesky photographer we all loved… until this year, anyway. "She's sneaky. You gotta keep your guard up, man." Antonio shook his head, but it was quickly forgotten when Buddy dropped off more beer, wings, onion rings, and sliders. "Thanks, Buddy."

We all dug into the food and refilled our glasses, silence reigning as we stuffed our faces, completely unaware of the world around us. While I ate, I debated telling the guys what had happened between me and Stevie. Not to brag, since I wasn't that guy, but because I needed some perspective.

"That photo looks like she's kind of your type," Ty remarked, completely out of the blue.

That was the perfect opening. "I didn't say I didn't like her, I said she wasn't my type." And both of those things were true. I couldn't explain it and I wasn't sure I wanted to understand it, but I couldn't keep denying it. "Something... happened."

The table fell silent for about a minute and then erupted into noise. Cheering and laughing, and I'm pretty sure Ty let out an excited whistle. "So, I guess she *is* your type. Eddy will be happy to hear that."

I pointed at my brother and sent him a threatening glare. "Tell her, and I'll make sure you have a target on your back until this calendar business is over." Fear brightened his eyes but Ty kept the *casual, not-worried-*at-all smile on his face.

"She'll find out eventually. It's not like this is a private place." Just to make his point, Ty glanced around the bar, which was even more packed than it had been an hour ago. "The question is, why would Eddy bring this Clara woman by if you already sealed the deal with your pretty assistant?"

I grunted and shook my head. "No, the question is why was Stevie completely not bothered *at all* by Eddy's overt attempts to match me with Clara?" I'd had a good time—hell, a great time—last night with Stevie, but her complete lack of concern was troubling. "She didn't appear jealous or angry. I'd say she was almost amused."

"Do you want more than sex with her?" Derek asked. "Because you've said that she wasn't your type. Twice."

"Sounds to me like maybe the good doctor is worried maybe she didn't have as much fun as he did." Antonio's smirk only angered me because it was a lie. And because he was taunting me.

"We both had a great time. I'm sure of it." I shook my head. "I just don't get it. She didn't get angry at me or Eddy, and once Clara was gone, she didn't even mention it."

"Did you bring it up? Or last night?"

I shook my head and frowned at my brother. "No. Why would I?"

"He's an idiot," Ty said, pointing at me as he stared at the other two. "A doctor, and an idiot."

"I'm right here. And I'm not an idiot."

They all laughed like this was the biggest damn joke they'd ever heard. Then Ty turned to me. "If you're not interested in more than one night with this woman *who isn't your type*, why does it matter how she reacted the morning after?"

It was a good question, and I didn't have a real answer for it. "I don't know, okay? I just wasn't ready for her easy acceptance of whatever the hell Eddy is up to now."

"Ahhh," Derek said around a mouthful of meat and onion rings. "You wanted Stevie to go all cavewoman on Clara and Eddy, pretend like she has some sort of claim on you? At the office, no less." He shook his head. "Never took you for one of those guys."

"I'm not," I barked, getting angry all over again.

"Good," Ty said with a smile. "Because Stevie just walked in." Every head at the table swiveled to the door, where she strolled through and greeted Buddy with an easy smile. "You could just go talk to her."

I could do that, but she didn't even give the bar a cursory glance, as if she really didn't give a damn who was inside because there was no one she wanted to see. Not even me, hell, maybe especially not me. "Maybe she's meeting someone." It was a weak answer, but I avoided saying more by shoving my face into my beer.

"He's scared," Ty announced, sounding way too damn amused. "Worried she'll tell the whole bar he didn't satisfy her properly."

Ty was trying to goad me and I refused to give in, even if my gaze kept sliding over to the woman in question, watching her chat amicably with Buddy but otherwise ignore the world around her.

"He's got it bad." Antonio's deep voice penetrated my thoughts, but I tuned them out as best I could because… because of Stevie.

Stevie, who was tough as nails on the outside but somehow managed to squeal like a little girl when Buddy brought out his favorite masterpiece, beef and black bean nachos, stacked with several layers of chips, extra guac and jalapeño peppers. She clapped, taking in the size of the plate with wide, excited eyes.

"See? He hasn't heard one single thing we've said for the past ten minutes. Yep, he's got it bad," Derek agreed with a laugh. "Maxine will be delighted to hear it."

That grabbed my attention, turning it away from the bar and back to the table. "You will *all* keep your damn mouths shut."

Despite my being bigger than all of them, they all laughed. Heads back, with fists banging on the table to draw the attention of everyone in Black Thumb. It was all one big joke. Ty whistled and shook his head. "Looks like it's been taken out of your hands. Tough luck, baby bro."

The smirk on his face drew my attention to the door but there was no one there, just a few women stumbling out together. But when my gaze turned to the bar, to Stevie, she was no longer on her own. "Rafe," I growled. The fire chief was a good guy. He was good-looking, according to all the women in town, and the whole fire-fighter thing was definitely a draw, but he didn't date and didn't seem to be looking for anything serious. He could break Stevie's heart.

"Rafe might be prettier than you, but you're still a catch." Ty clapped me on the back with a sympathetic smile. "And he's only made her laugh, what, *three* times since he sat down."

"Just a couple minutes ago," Antonio added, pouring more salt into a wound that shouldn't even exist.

I knew what they were doing, but no matter how much I talked myself out of it, my body wouldn't listen. The legs of my chair scraped against the floor as I pushed it back too fast, nearly toppling it. I caught it in time, righted the chair and set Stevie in my sights. "I'll be right back."

Behind me, laughter and cheers sounded, but I ignored it all. I had a woman to see about.

"So, did you become a firefighter because chicks dig them, or do you have a hero complex?" Rafe Montgomery was the fire chief, and the man looked like he belonged in the movies. On the big billboard and everything. He had thick, dark brown hair that was almost black, and light brown eyes that looked gold in some lights, especially when he was holding in laughter.

"A hero complex?" His lips curled into a charming smile I was sure set plenty of hearts on fire. "Haven't you heard? I'm an actual hero."

He was attractive and charming, but there was no spark anywhere in sight. Still, I tossed my head back and laughed. "So, you're one of the guys Janey convinced to go shirtless for charity?"

Rafe leaned in and stole one of my nachos, deep rumbling laughter erupting when I smacked his hand away. "If I say yes, are you gonna go out and pre-order one?"

I tapped my chin and grinned. "Maybe. I mean, the rest of the heroes are pretty hot, too, so if there's just one dud, at least it's for charity." Rafe was just what I needed after a long day of reminding myself that I didn't do jealousy. Ever. At all. He was entertaining eye candy, which was, frankly, the best kind.

He laughed again and stole another nacho. "Damn, these are good. And the perfect way to make up for being so mean."

I frowned. "I wasn't mean enough to share my nachos with you, Chief."

Rafe shrugged and ordered a beer as Buddy walked past. "Where's a little thing like you gonna put all this food?"

"I'll find a place, Rafe, don't you worry." I had a healthy metabolism, and running around Scott's office all day was an excellent calorie burner. Not to mention the Tuesday and Thursday runs to local farms and ranches, which included plenty of physical activity.

"Am I interrupting?" Scott's deep voice boomed between us, sounding jealous and unhappy. A quick look in the mirror behind the bar revealed he was both.

"Yes," I said sharply.

"Nope," Rafe said at the same time, giving me a look that said he didn't want to get in the middle of whatever the hell was on Scott's mind.

"Actually, we were in the middle of an entertaining conversation. How can I help you, Scott?"

He blinked, like he didn't understand why his macho pissing routine wasn't working. "We need to talk."

Rafe stood with an apologetic grin. "Catch you later, Stevie."

My shoulders fell, not because I wanted Rafe to stay but because I didn't want any part of the thunderous expression on Scott's face. "Next time, I might even share my nachos with you."

He laughed and gave my shoulder a light squeeze as he passed, stopping to whisper in my ear. "Don't be too hard on him, he's a good guy. And if that picture on Facebook is anything to go by, you think so, too."

Picture? "What picture?"

Rafe laughed and turned to Scott. "I'll let Scott tell you all about it." He grinned and walked away, joining Ty and a couple other men at a table nearby.

We stared at each other for a long time, too many emotions swirling between us for any type of communication to take place, so I turned back to my nachos and dug in.

He sat beside me, quietly, for a long moment. Finally, he said what he'd come to say. "About Clara. I don't know her, and I don't give a damn about her."

Okay. It wasn't what I'd expected, so I shrugged. "All right, but you don't owe me an explanation." We'd had one really excellent night together, but that was it.

He looked genuinely confused and for a second, I almost felt sorry for him. "So, that's it? One and done?"

I barked out a laugh. "That's rich, coming from the guy who snuck out in the middle of the night."

"It was early morning, and I needed to get my run in and take care of Hershey."

Okay, that *was* perfectly reasonable. "How was I supposed to know that? And what was I supposed to think?"

Buddy stopped in front of us with a smile. "Everything all right?"

"Yep." The word came out a little too bright and my smile was brittle—at least, it felt that way to me. "Peachy keen."

"Keep it that way," he barked and walked away.

Scott sighed when Buddy left. "I wasn't sure what to say or do, and Hershey was the perfect excuse to leave. I'm sorry."

Now *that* shocked the hell out of me. "Are you sure now?"

"What?"

"You barged over here all angry and possessive like you have any right, so I assume you've figured out what to say or do?" He didn't look all that certain, and I had a feeling he'd only come over because the handsome fire chief was flirting with me.

Scott laughed. "I had all day to figure it out and I got nothing. Sorry." He grabbed my beer and took a long, fortifying gulp, finishing with a satisfied smack of his lips. "I had a great time, Stevie. It was unexpected and it was incredible. But…" He trailed off, but it didn't take a genius to figure out the rest of that sentence.

"But I work for you, and even *that's* up in the air," I finished for him. Scott was definitely a rule follower, a disciple of etiquette and good behavior. "Don't worry,

Scotty, I won't sue you when you fire me. I know those are two separate things."

He sucked in a breath, searching for the words to make this awkwardness better. The problem was, there were no words—sometimes things were just... what they were.

"See you in the morning." I slapped a twenty-dollar bill on the bar to cover my beer, nachos, and tip, and slid off the stool. "I had a good time, too, Scott, but I know what this is. I know the difference between desire and compatibility. You *want* me but you don't want to. Some days, I'm not even sure you really like me, but whatever. It was fun and I don't need it to be more than that."

Maybe a small, teensy little part of me had been hoping for more, but I gave up on clinging to hope after my mom died. And I left behind that hope with Scott when I walked out of Black Thumb.

SCOTT

I was just about halfway through another tense yet highly efficient day at the office. If having her around wasn't so good for business and for my peace of mind, I'd get rid of her for making me second-guess myself. If she wasn't so unfailingly polite, I might actually have a legitimate reason to get rid of her. If I really wanted to, which I didn't.

Dammit.

It didn't take a genius to figure out she was mad at me, but I'd gotten used to her straight-forward ways. I never had to worry about what Stevie was thinking, because she would tell me if I needed to know. Except, now, she didn't say anything that wasn't work related, and I didn't know what the hell to think about that. And the worst part was that nothing I did worked. Not splurging on that stupid sugary coffee drink all the women in town seemed to lose their heads over—that had earned me a small smile and a soft-spoken 'thank you'. A big ol' greasy breakfast didn't even warrant a full smile. At least the utterly gluttonous dinner of pizza and a gyro I'd brought her was met with a toothy grin. But, as of yet, nothing I did or said had cracked Stevie's armor.

A knock sounded at the door and the woman who had been doing a pretty good imitation of someone who *hadn't* seen me naked strolled in with a serious expression on her face. "What's up, Stevie?"

She sucked in an almost silent breath that came out on a rush. "We have a walk-in, a pony." At my wide-eyed expression, she continued on, unfazed. "Yes, a real pony. Apparently, Mikey Ford spotted the poor thing on his way to 'The Dairy Farm' for a class field trip." She used finger quotes, because she didn't know Tulip shorthand. Yet. "Anyway, he called Penny, who called Ry, who called in a favor, and now Betty is here. With the pony."

That sounded like an average day in town, and I stood with a smile. "Welcome to Tulip, Stevie."

"Hmph." That was her only response and before I could ask what she meant by that, Stevie was gone, as if she couldn't even stand to be in the same room with me.

A quick look at the time said I had twenty minutes before my next scheduled appointment, so I finished my cup of coffee and went to Betty and the pony in the large animal exam room. "Afternoon, Betty. What have we got here?" The pony was black all over, with black hair that would be shiny once it had been washed and cared for properly.

"My grandson called, frantic that the poor thing looked sick and all alone, so what could I do?" She shrugged, a content smile on her face. Though Mike wasn't hers biologically, Betty spoiled him rotten as if he was her own. "Looks all right. Seen better days, but nothing he can't come back from. Isn't that right, boy?"

The pony was subdued and easygoing. I already knew a few places who would be happy to have him. "Any plans for what you'll do with him once he's got a clean bill of health?"

Betty laughed and shrugged as she crossed her arms and got comfortable in the hard plastic chair. "I figured you could tell me what my options are. And then maybe I could tell you the same."

My shoulders fell in disappointment. I couldn't believe that I hadn't seen this ploy coming a mile away. I stood, with one hand still on the pony, and glared at the older woman. "Where did you even find this pony?"

This time, she let out a raucous, full-throated laugh. "I just volunteered to bring him over when this opportunity presented itself. Now, do you want to listen to me or argue with me? I'm good either way."

Like I actually had a choice. If it wasn't Betty right now, it would be someone else at another place and another time. "Fine. Talk." I listened to most of what Betty had to say while I looked over the pony, which didn't take very long at all.

"Things seem like they've cooled off with you and Stevie." It wasn't a question, and I frowned.

"You've got faulty intel, Betty. Things were never all that hot to begin with." They could have been—hell, they *would* have been, if Stevie wasn't so stubborn. So determined to deny this thing between us, when I couldn't.

"Despite that photo on the Facebook?" Both brows rose in silver arches that said *you're full of it*. "If you say so. I guess now we have our answer on how a handsome doctor and former NFL player could still be single. Idiocy." Betty shook her head and smacked her lips together. "I had higher hopes for you, Scott."

"I haven't done a damn thing wrong," I insisted defiantly. If this was what it meant to be in a relationship, taking blame for something I hadn't done, then I didn't want any part of it.

"You haven't done anything right, either, by the sounds of things." Betty shook her head and smiled at the pony, rubbing his matted mane. "You both look pissed off and in need of a long weekend in bed, if you know what I'm sayin'."

"I groaned. "It'd be hard not to know what you're saying, Betty."

"Smart ass," she said, and pointed me like she was chastising a child. "Look, maybe you kids do things differently today, but some things don't change—and one of those things is that a woman likes to be wooed. She might need to be wooed differently, 'cause I don't think dinner and a movie or dinner and dancing will work on Stevie, but a rock concert or a tattoo convention? You can figure out something that floats her boat." Betty made it sound simple, but she hadn't been pressed up against the brick wall that was Stevie when she was determined to be stubborn. "If she has fun, then maybe she'll start to think about how to float your boat." Then she laughed to herself, so proud of her innuendo that it even tugged a reluctant smile across my face.

I groaned and dropped my face into one hand. "Betty, please." I finished up with the pony and made arrangements to keep him housed in a free stable out back for a day or two. "We wouldn't have worked anyway, Betty, so it's a good thing you ladies got it all wrong. At least now we can have a good professional relationship."

There was something about the way Betty arched her brow, or maybe it was the mischief that sparkled in the dark depths of her eyes, but her skepticism had me worried. "You think so?"

I would never show that kind of weakness, especially not to the wannabe matchmakers in town. "Absolutely." My chest puffed out and I spoke that one word with the kind of confidence, the kind of smugness you just knew would come back to bite you in the ass sooner rather than later.

"Good for you." With a sympathetic smile—the one polite southern women reserved for idiots and simpletons —and a pat to the shoulder, Betty left me, quite literally, holding the pony. She was out the door before I could come up with something else to say.

I wasn't sure how much longer I could take Scott's torture. What the hell was wrong with the man that he couldn't just be normal? Couldn't just keep his distance and pretend like we never got naked and did the butt-naked boogie together? As much as my ego would love to believe that I'd rocked his world so thoroughly that he now couldn't get enough of me, I wasn't a complete fool. A man who couldn't get enough of you didn't scram out of bed before he got morning-after seconds. I was pretty sure that was an actual rule, written down somewhere and everything.

It was hard enough when he accidentally pressed in too close and I caught a whiff of his masculine scent that was an odd blend of sandalwood, leather, animals and... lemons. One whiff of that smell was usually accompanied by visions of his square jaw clenched tight when he was holding back his own pleasure until I drank my fill. Didn't he have any idea just how hard I was working to resist him and to keep things strictly professional between us?

"Excuse me? I'm here to see Dr. Henderson." Clara beamed a smile down at me that I was sure often got her whatever she wanted, from Broadway tickets to access to all kinds of clubs, premieres, and openings. "Does he have a free moment to see me?" She batted her eyelashes, keeping her spine straight to highlight her tiny waist and the perfectly sculpted curve of her tits. They were worth whatever they cost.

A damn professional, that's what I am. I repeated those words to myself several times and slapped a smile on my face before hitting Clara with it. "Do you have an appointment?"

"I don't. Unfortunately." Clara giggled and instead of being annoyed, I was in awe. She somehow managed to make a giggle sound like a purr from a grown woman instead of a teeny-bopper. "But I'm hoping he's willing to make time to squeeze me in."

Someone needed to tell this chick that innuendo was best when used on the person you wanted to get naked with. Not his assistant. But since correcting her wasn't part of my job, I flashed an even brighter smile and turned back to my computer screen and the scheduling software. "Let's see what I can do. Now?"

"That would be ideal, but I'm flexible." This was a woman who didn't play around. I admired that she had no problem or shame going after exactly what she wanted. Or who. Today, Clara wore a hot pink dress that fit each and every one of her curves, showing off her cinched waist and long legs. It was proof she never said yes to carbs and exercised religiously. The woman was just about perfect and, unlike mere mortals like myself, she knew how close she came to the mark. "Very flexible."

"Obvious, too," Betty Kemp said, doing a terrible job of using her inside voice.

"Excellent. I'll find the first free slot."

"Thanks," she said at the same time Scott's deep voice growled.

"Free slot for what?" His deep voice tore me away from cataloguing all of Clara's perfections while I found a fifteen-minute window for her to make her play for Scott.

"Clara needs an appointment with you for an undefined reason, and I'm searching the calendar to fit her flexibility." I looked up at him and dared him to say one damn word. "It looks like you're done with Betty, now could work."

"Perfect." Clara beamed and took two wide steps until she was at Scott's side, one arm snaking its way around his bigger, harder one.

Caught, Scott glared at me and I knew he and I would have words later, when the office was empty. For now, I was determined to enjoy his discomfort. "I guess we can take a look now. Where's Ivory?" Scott looked around, along with both me and Betty, and found the little yapping monster was nowhere in sight.

Clara laughed. "I figured we could do a quick consult. I'll tell you her symptoms and you tell me if she needs to come in. If so, I'll bring her in later." The heat in that last word was enough to singe my eyelashes, yet Scott seemed wholly unimpressed.

"You do consults now, do you, Scotty?" The amusement in Betty's voice was like a palpable thing in the air. "Wait until I tell the girls." The glare he sent her had no effect, other than making her laugh even louder and with her whole body. "So long, guys. Be sure to take good care of that pony, because I'm sure Mikey will want to see him soon." With a quick finger wave, Betty was gone, leaving the tense exchange down to three players.

Clara cleared her throat and pressed her body up against Scott's. So, do you have time for me now?" She batted her eyelashes expertly and even I wasn't sure how Scott hadn't already fallen completely under her spell, especially when she did that practiced bite-down on her bottom lip. It was pure sex appeal. "It'll only take a moment. I promise."

Scott's gaze landed on me, as if I held some power to extract him from the situation. His glare was heavy enough that I felt the burden of it on my shoulders before he turned to Clara. "Sorry, but now isn't great. I just got a pony and I have to find a place to lodge him for a night or two." A big fat lie, since there were stables and other enclosures out back just in case we needed to keep animals for observation. Before she could talk him out of it, Scott stalked away.

Weird. "You want me to put you on the books, Clara?"

She glared, like it was my fault he wasn't catching what she was so obviously tossing out. "No. I'll catch him around. He can't run from me forever," she said ominously and left.

Finally alone with my thoughts, I sat there for at least a full minute, maybe twenty of them, wondering what in the hell had just happened. Scott seemed like he wanted me to be jealous and was upset that I wasn't, and was turning down a gorgeous sure thing who was, let's face it, right up his alley. It didn't make sense and trying to figure it out was giving me a headache, until I remembered none of this was my problem and I got back to work.

It was amazing just how busy a small town vet's office was from one day to the next. It wasn't just for things like vaccinations and birth control, which I'd expected, but people brought in cats with colds, dogs with diabetes, and birds with a possible gluten allergy. I was busier than I ever thought I would be at the clinic, and that was just how I liked it.

Especially now.

"That wasn't funny." His big body cast a dark shadow across my keyboard and computer screen before his words interrupted my train of thought. "You know, just in case you thought it was." I didn't need to turn around or lean back to know how close he was; I could *feel* his near-ness, his warmth. The invisible pull he seemed to have over me.

I let my gaze climb his body slowly, taking my time to look my fill of his narrow waist and straight hips, those wide, capable shoulders and his massive chest. It was hard to pull my eyes away. When my gaze landed on his face, I looked away quickly, refusing to get snared in his web.

"What wasn't funny?" There was something about Scott that brought my inner child to the surface, and I couldn't help but poke at him. Constantly.

"That thing you pulled with Cara."

"Clara," I corrected automatically. "And don't even think about blaming that on me. I have no idea what you do with your free time, and it's not my job to know. She wanted an appointment and my job is to book your appointments."

He leaned down low, resting on his forearms until his face was inches from mine. "You're a bad liar."

I shrugged. "Maybe I am. Or maybe you're a suspicious person? You never stopped to consider that, did you?"

He laughed and it was good laugh, rich and well used, deep and sincere. "I did, actually. But that doesn't turn you into some world-class liar. Do you make it a habit of pushing your conquests off on other women?" His arms were folded and there was a smile on his face, but the burning intensity in his eyes said my answer mattered to him.

Conquests? I couldn't help but laugh at that old-fashioned phrasing. "No. But I am also *not* in the habit of turning into a crazy woman over a man who clearly is not interested. If that's your kink, I think Clara might be more up your alley than you realize." The woman looked like she wouldn't be above boiling a bunny or engaging in a little light stalking if it got her what she wanted.

His expression changed, darkened. "I don't want Clara."

"Interesting." My tone said I wasn't interested at all, but I was. I really, really was.

His green gaze intensified, and I felt it all the way down to my tingling toes. I swallowed hard, grateful to be sitting down. "There's someone else who has snagged my attention."

"Interesting," I said again, because what the hell else could I say? "Maybe you should be telling her this, not me." My heart raced and even though he hadn't given me confirmation it was me, my lips fought my willpower to keep the coming smile at bay.

Scott's own smile flashed as wide as the sun and his big hand landed in a hard smack against the desk. "You know, maybe I will." Then he turned and walked away. Whistling cheerfully.

What in the hell had just happened?

"*I*t's my day off." Stevie tried to scowl up at me, but the squint from the sun shining in her face over my shoulder ruined the effect.

My gaze roamed her body on its own, taking in hard nipples before making its way to perky breasts hidden behind a thin tank top that gave way to a slender waist before her hips flared out, tempting me. The shirt ended just high enough to tell me she was also wearing black panties. "Is this how you always answer the door?"

Stevie's gaze shifted from my face down to her body and then back up with a shrug. "Everything is covered. What do you want?"

Loaded question. "What are you up to today?"

"Why?"

Seriously? "Just answer the damn question."

Surprisingly, she rolled her violet eyes and let out a put-upon sigh before she answered. "Nothing, okay? I'm going to sleep in and maybe go for a walk. Enjoy my *day off."* My lips twitched and her scowl returned. "Something funny, Scotty?"

"Nope, not at all." I don't know why I found her so amusing, but it certainly explained why I was standing on her doorstep early on a Saturday morning. "Feel like taking a drive?"

She blinked and folded her arms across her chest, which I really wished she hadn't done because it put her breasts on full display. "With you?"

It was my turn for the eyeroll. "No, the captain of the football team asked me to ask you in homeroom, but I figured it couldn't wait."

Her lips twitched and I knew I had her. "Yeah? Who is this captain guy?"

"Me."

Her gaze went dark and glazed over for a second as she took in my body, as if seeing me for the first time. "I figured you for a high school jock. Where are we driving, and is this a one-way trip for one of us?"

I blinked, twice and frowned. "What?"

"You're not planning on taking me on a long walk off a short pier, are you?" Stevie arched her eyebrows, expression deadly serious, and I took a step back.

"What? No!"

Her shoulders fell dramatically. "Okay. If you say so," she said, so sarcastically I wanted to make her squirm. I took a step forward. A big step. "So, where is it, *exactly*, that you want me to go with you?"

"A friend's farm. I'd like to show it to you, and then we'll have lunch with them." That was almost the whole story.

Stevie looked at me, suspicion burning in her eyes, but I saw the moment she gave in. "Is this a work thing, or can I wear regular clothes?"

"What you're wearing is perfect to me." A little *too* perfect, if the tightness in my jeans was anything to go by. "But I'm no fashion expert."

"What time?"

"Thirty minutes?"

Another put-upon sigh. "If I'm ready by then, I'll go." A perfect non-committal answer, if I ever heard one.

I accepted it, because I wouldn't let Stevie get to me. Not today. I wanted her to see... hell, I didn't really know what I wanted her to see, but I wanted her to see me, dammit. She could put up walls all she wanted, but it hadn't helped me stop wanting her, and I was pretty sure it wouldn't help her stop wanting me, either.

I showed up twenty-five minutes later, hopeful. "Ready?"

"You're annoying, you know that?"

"I know you don't mean it, so my feelings aren't hurt. And because I have iced tea and croissants stuffed with cheese in the truck."

"You should have led with that," she said before turning away and pushing the door closed.

I stopped it before it closed completely and stepped inside. "Food is more compelling than my company?"

Stevie froze and looked over her shoulder, one dark brow arched questioningly. "Did I invite you in?"

"Not directly, but you left the door open." In more ways than one.

"Did it take you all morning to think of that?" she asked, shoving her feet into a pair of purple canvas sneakers.

"Nope. Just now, in fact."

Stevie grabbed a colorful wallet with geometric shapes all over it, oddly out of character, and stared blankly at me. "Congratulations." When she shooed me out, I took advantage of the space and smiled. Stevie was tough when she wanted to be, but her response now gave me hope that today might help me crack the shell she'd put around herself. "It smells incredible in here." She grabbed the bag and jumped into the truck, ignoring my outstretched hand in favor of the bag's contents.

"Yeah, no problem," I mumbled to myself unnecessarily. I should be happy that she doesn't stand on ceremony like that, but for some reason, it annoyed me. "You don't like letting people help you, do you?"

My question stopped her movements and she stared at me, a little crinkle of confusion forming between her black brows. "When I need help, I ask for it."

There was no point arguing the point because I realized she probably didn't even realize I was trying to help her, so I started the engine and we got on the road. "Sure would be nice to eat that croissant while it's still warm."

"I know," she said around a smiling mouthful. "You probably should have eaten yours before you started driving." I turned and stared at her in disbelief for as long as

I could safely keep my eyes off the road. Her laughter rang out and echoed inside the car. "Goodness, that look was totally worth the risk." She chuckled to herself before breaking off a piece and holding it up to my lips. "Open up."

I ignored her playful sing-song voice and opened my mouth, swiping my tongue across her fingertip when she lingered a little too long. "Thanks."

"No problem," she bit out, hoping her anger would disguise the desire.

"It's okay to feel it, Stevie. I feel it, too." It was a risk, but that swift intake of breath told me more than the silence that followed.

"You know people who live here?"

"I'll try not to take offense to your tone."

She shrugged and ducked to take in every detail as we passed. "The Peace Community? You are definitely not the crunchy-granola-hippie type and, considering your reaction to me, I can't imagine you'd think of them as friends."

I hated to admit that she had me there. "This is a unique friendship that was born out of necessity." We both stepped from the car and I watched her as she took in the farm, eyes darting from the flower garden on the sunny side of the house to the horses in a pasture in the distance.

Just then, Star stepped out onto the wide widow's porch that I'd helped her paint one summer a few years ago. She looked every bit the crunchy-granola-hippie type Stevie had pictured, with her waist-length blond hair that now had more gray in it and a paisley patterned dress that fell straight to the ground, highlighting her rail-thin frame. "Scott, it's so good to see you again. It's been too long."

I opened my arms and accepted Star's hug. The woman was affectionate with everyone, though as beautiful as she was it was always maternal. But I still enjoyed the flash of jealousy I glimpsed in Stevie's eyes. "It's good to see you too, Star. Still getting too lost in painting to remember to eat, I see."

She laughed and turned to Stevie. "I'm Star, and this is The Peace Community. Welcome."

"It's gorgeous. A lot of work, I'm sure."

"Tons, but it's rewarding to know that all of our sweat, and sometimes tears, is going towards nourishing our bodies and the community around us."

I held my breath and waited for Stevie to mock Star the way I once had, but she merely shrugged. "Admirable. Do you notice a real difference in your energy and stress levels?"

Star's eyes flashed with hope and happiness as she stepped closer to Stevie. "Absolutely. I'll tell you all about my own transformation, but I'll tell you what I tell everyone. Give it thirty days and if you feel good, give it another thirty. Keep going until it stops working for you." She threaded her arm through Stevie's and turned to me. "You brought a friend."

"I did."

"I hope that's okay," Stevie added. "He didn't exactly give me any details."

"Is that so?" Star's lips curled into a mischievous smile

that suddenly had me reconsidering my plan for the day. "Interesting."

"What is?" Stevie asked, anger underlying those two simple words.

"Nothing," Star said quickly. "Shall we go check on the animals?" Before anyone could object or ask questions, she herded us toward the pens, starting with the three horses in the pasture and then a couple of rescue pigs before moving on to two old goats.

"What kind of farm is this?"

Star laughed. "It's a regular vegetable and fruit farm, though Andre is experimenting with vegan cheese at the moment. The animals are part of our rescue program and soon, hopefully, Scott will start up the sister program."

I groaned at her not-so-subtle reminder. "Things like that take time, Star. You know that better than anybody."

"And without your help, I might not ever have gotten it to where it is today, which is why I'm pushing you now. Is it money you need?"

That was a nice start. "What I need is twelve more hours in the day." And more money, I had to admit, to rehab the structures to house the animals properly. And to hire staff to oversee everything. "A topic we can talk about later."

Stevie's ebony brows rose at my harsh tone, but Star laughed it off with a dismissive wave of her hands. "Fine. We have a newbie, an overbred mini horse named D'Artagnan with a limp. Let me know what you think?" I nodded and she smiled. "Excellent. Stevie can help me in the kitchen while I tell her all about my farm diet."

I shook my head as the women headed off, taking comfort in the silence and the company of the animals. It was one of the reasons I enjoyed coming here, and why I'd needed to come this weekend. These were all rescue animals, yet despite the cruelty and neglect they'd suffered, they were all loving and sweet, eagerly offering up hugs and kisses, sometimes in hopes of a treat. Star had hired me to help when no one was interested in an inexperienced vet fresh out of school, and I tried to make it out here at least once a month to look at the animals and catch up with everyone.

As I checked on my charges, I wondered what secrets Star had managed to get out of Stevie—and wondered how I could bribe her to share them with me.

STEVIE

"So, how long have you and Scott been together?" Star asked the question so casually, she'd almost gotten me to relax. Almost.

"Together? We're not—at least, not how you mean. I'm his assistant," I told her and gave her a quick rundown of our crazy meeting. "I'm new to town and he's being a good southern boy."

Star's laugh came out melodic and feminine, which only made the sibling vibe she and Scott gave off all the more baffling. "I don't know you well, but even I can tell you don't believe that. I think you could be good for Scott —and he thinks so, too, or else you wouldn't be here."

I shrugged, ignoring that feeling in my chest that felt a little like hope. "I didn't have anything else to do today and I was bribed. With pastries."

"What did Scott tell you about this place?"

"Almost nothing," I admitted, just to prove how uninvolved Scott and I were. "Just that he was coming out to a friend's farm."

"I was desperate for cheap vet help when I started this place, and Scott was fresh out of school. He worked hard, long hours, too, but he never said no to any of the animals —to the point that other people started bringing their animals here for treatment." She laughed at the memory. "Finally, I told him it was time to go out into the world. Kicked him off the ranch and gave him a nice retainer, just in case he got too busy for an old friend."

I ignored the relief I felt at hearing they were never lovers. It wasn't my business or my problem, even if they had been. "You're a good friend."

"I am, and he's been a good friend to me, too, but he hasn't been by for one of our Saturday lunches in quite some time. I'm guessing you have something to do with that."

I didn't know what Star meant, so I shrugged. Scott was a grown man who did what he wanted; I didn't factor into that at all. "Doubtful. I assist him in the field, so it makes sense he'd want me close by."

Star stared at me for so long I started to squirm in discomfort, then she shook her head with a small smile on her lips, shaped like a cupid's bow. "I can't tell if you're just in denial or if you really don't see what I saw in just a few minutes."

"That's sexual tension, nothing more."

"If you say so. Mash these potatoes for me, will ya?" Star hefted a pot that was half my height onto the counter and turned away, returning moments later with butter, salt, pepper, herbs, and a potato masher. "Thanks."

I got quite the upper-body workout mashing and seasoning the potatoes while Star danced around the kitchen preparing at least half a dozen dishes. An hour or more later, we sat down to eat with nearly a dozen people. "All of you live here?"

They all nodded. "Some have their own homes on the property, but most of us live here. There's plenty of room and this place is ninety percent off-grid," Star informed me proudly.

"Ninety? Last time I was here, it was only eighty," Scott said, awe in his voice.

"You've been gone a long time," the man named Andre said to him, sounding none too happy about it.

"Setting up a new practice is a lot of work." The tension between the men was thick and threatened to derail all the hard work Star and the others had put into the feast currently laid out on the table.

"Made harder when you refuse to hire an assistant," I grumbled and looked at Scott with wide eyes, hoping he got my message.

Andre laughed. "Heaven forbid he ask anyone for help."

I turned accusing eyes on Scott. "I guess that was more than just a little bit of projection."

He laughed and shook his head. "I have no idea what you're talking about." At his words, the table erupted in laughter and I kept a smile on my face while I ate and listened to their stories, watching the way they interacted.

I envied their easy camaraderie; it was something I hadn't really bothered stopping to make time for since I'd left the family ranch behind, always working and saving for a rainy day. Connections and friendships had been the first thing to go when I left, and it didn't seem like a priority since I never knew how long I'd stick in one place. They were loud and colorful and all up in each other's business, but they were a family.

It was nice.

"Don't let them fool you, they're all crazy," Scott whispered in my ear.

I gave him a sideways glance and a smile. "Seems to me that you like crazy more than you let on."

"Maybe you're right," he agreed ominously and dug into his second, or maybe it was his third pile of mashed potatoes.

The afternoon passed in a blur of food and wine for me, soda for Scott, and so much conversation I'd be happy to sit in silence for the next week or two. It was nice, though, more than nice. Too bad it had me thinking of Scott as something more than my stick-in-the-mud boss. Hell, I was even thinking of him as more than a sex object. Dammit.

"You're awful quiet over there. Something on your mind?" Scott's voice came out on a loud echo inside the silent vehicle.

"Just thinking. Are you satisfied with your payments?" Unbelievably, Scott had accepted a variety of artisan products ranging from pickles, vegan cheese, preserves, blueberry wine, and strawberry liqueur—all organic and healthy as hell—in lieu of cold, hard cash. It was amazing, really, and only served to reveal more of his human side to me.

"Damn happy, especially with the banana bread. That stuff is perfect for breakfast and dessert. I'll even give you one, for keeping Andre off my case." He shook his head. "They always come up with the best stuff."

"Why did you invite me today?"

He shrugged. "I wanted you to see another side of me, I guess."

Mission accomplished, but it still didn't make any sense. "Why?"

He let out a loud, barking laugh. "Now who's being suspicious?"

Me. And rightly so. "What's going on in that head of yours?"

He battled his eyelashes at me. "Don't you mean my pretty little head?"

Somehow, he managed to tease another smile out of me. "You need me to tell you that you're pretty, Scott?" I leaned in, batting my eyelashes until they fluttered. "You're very pretty, Scotty."

"You ruined it," he groaned and shouldered me away, tugging another laugh out of me.

"Sorry," I told him, sounding about as apologetic as I felt, which was not at all.

"Right," he snorted and fell silent once again. He was hard to read—flirty and friendly one moment, and cool and aloof the next. It was a game I didn't enjoy, no matter how much I wanted him.

Which was just further confirmation that I needed to keep ignoring whatever this *thing* was between us. I turned to look out the passenger window, watching the Texas countryside fly by in a beautiful flash of colors.

"Remember that woman I told you I was interested in?"

I nodded, sure he was about to reveal it was Star all along.

"Well, it's you." Scott said the words simply, like it was news I should have expected to hear. Which was crazy since he had Clara chasing him down, and he'd made it clear how he felt when he ran from my bed. "Feel free to say something. Anything."

I wanted to, but I couldn't. What could I possibly say, when a hot doctor tells me he wants me? "Why me?" was the only question that came to mind. We didn't have anything in common, and sophisticated women like Clara were more up his alley, not mouthy assistants with too many tattoos. "It doesn't make sense."

But Scott only laughed, like it was all some joke. "I've already made these same arguments to myself over the past few weeks. They aren't working."

I sighed, cursing him for voicing my concerns. "And?"

"And I'm done fighting it. I want you and you want me, apparently that's all that matters, so..."

"So, what?"

"So, I'm in. I'm willing to do this. Me and you." The words sounded even more dramatic when the car came to a stop and he shifted into park. The instant silence engulfed us as the engine died in front of his house. "What do you say?"

What did I say? I had no words yet, so I stepped out of the car and started down the paved path to the guest house. "I don't know."

Scott fell into step beside me and shrugged. "You know, but you don't want to say it."

He was right, I was being a coward—and I was no damn coward. "We're not right for each other. I'm not sure you really even like me half the time, and I'm not changing who I am for anyone."

He sighed, a smile playing around his lips. "Good, because I'm not asking you to, Stevie. All I'm asking you to do is give us a shot. We'll go on a few dates, talking late while drinking too much, and see what happens. What do you say?"

I sighed and turned to Scott, my back against the door —I was literally caught between a rock of a chest, and a hard place. And I couldn't think of anywhere else I wanted to be. Or anyone else I wanted to be with. "I say, *what the hell*," I told him and flung my body into his, smashing my lips against his until he caught on and wrapped his arms around me.

At some point, somehow, we made it inside before our clothes came off, and we spent the rest of the afternoon and evening in bed.

SCOTT

*T*here was nothing better in the whole wide world than waking up with a soft, willing woman in your arms. It didn't matter that it wasn't quite morning yet, or that the soft, willing woman was still asleep with her ass pressed against my growing erection, her back flush against my chest and her thick black waves covering my face. Her hair smelled like honey, and her skin smelled like sweat and sex. And vanilla.

I had to have a taste.

Leaning forward until the warmth of her body heated my lips, I wrapped one arm around her waist as the other hand closed around the closest breast before I started peppering the back of her neck with kisses. A soft groan escaped but she wasn't fully awake, not yet. Slowly, as if I had the time in the world, I kissed my way down her spine until she shivered and moaned.

It was that moan that was like a bow of lust straight to

my cock. Heat surged through me, filling my veins with fire, as her back arched into me and I knew the moment she woke up because it was the moment my tongue slipped inside her wet heat and a low, strangled moan escaped from her pouty lips. One hand gripped the bed sheets and the other reached around and found a handful of my hair.

Stevie didn't say much, she just moaned and cried out her pleasure, nothing more than brief commands, like "More," and "Yes," and my personal favorite, "Please."

I lapped her up, sliding one finger deep as I tasted every part of her until she begged me, with her body, to stop. Only then did I tease her a little more until she crawled to get away from me, moaning as I held her still and sucked her clit until a second, more powerful orgasm burst out of her on a long, keening wail.

The sound kept me hard and aching as I slowly kissed my way up her body. "Good morning." Her lips split into a smile that I couldn't help but steal a taste of and when Stevie moaned into me, I pressed against where she was soaking wet and throbbing.

When I pulled back, she let out a husky laugh. "Best way to wake up. Ever."

"Can't argue with that," I groaned when her legs slipped around my waist, pulling me even closer. "More importantly, I don't want to." Her hand snaked between our overheated bodies and wrapped around my cock, putting me exactly where she wanted me.

"Finally, something you won't argue with me about."

I laughed but it was the last coherent sound I made for

a good long while, because slipping inside of her tight heat once again was like heaven. She was so hot, her pale skin flushed with desire as she tossed her head back and arched into me, putting rosy red nipples within tasting distance. My tongue flicked against her nipple before I pulled it into my mouth, sucking hard as her body clamped hard around mine, the aftershocks of her last orgasm still sending electricity through her body. It was a damn sight to behold.

"Scott," she moaned, digging her nails into my shoulders. "More, please."

"Greedy," I grunted out and sat up, gripping her hips hard and pulling her close until the angle was perfect to send her out of her mind. Stevie gripped my wrists, her violet gaze focused on nothing but me as I pounded into her body like I was the center of her world. Heat continued to surge through me at the desire in her eyes, at the way her lips were shiny and swollen from my kisses.

"Scott," she moaned again and again, each time the word came out lower, deeper, more desperate. "Scott," she growled and her fingers dug deeper into my flesh but I didn't give a damn because watching her fall apart first thing in the morning, as the first rays of sun filtered in, was worth a few battle scars. Stevie let out a strangled cry as her body clamped down hard around my cock, pulsing until she pulled my orgasm out to dance with hers.

My body shook and trembled, vibrated with too much energy as pleasure coursed through my veins and sweat dripped from my forehead. It was a powerful orgasm, explosive enough to blur my vision. "Oh… fuck!"

Even as shivers wracked her body, Stevie was still a smart ass. "Okay, so maybe three orgasms is the *best* way to wake up." Laughter shook her body and mine as her legs tightened around my waist like she wasn't eager to let me go. Suddenly, her expression went serious and her fingers threaded through my hair, then her lips were on mine in a hungry, intense kiss that set me on fire all over again.

"Happy to help." The words came out breathless but I didn't give a damn; Stevie's smiling lips somehow tasted sweetest of all.

"Good, because I could use a little bit more help." Her smiling lips touched mine once again and we sat like that for I didn't know how long, bodies meshed together, lips fused, and we kissed like horny teenagers until the sun lit up the whole room. The whole damn guest house. Stevie was as hot as a flame, licking my lips and sucking my tongue like a woman possessed.

I was already growing hard again, grinding up against her as we kissed and kissed.

"He didn't answer his door, but maybe she will." That voice was too familiar—and not one I wanted to hear when I was rocking a semi-chub.

"Or maybe he didn't answer because she was in there with him. Or he's in there with her," said Janey, the ironic voice of reason.

"If they're together, then maybe we shouldn't disturb them at all." Gotta love Eddy, always with her eye on the prize.

Stevie and I looked at each other, barely able to hold in

the laughter. "If we're really quiet, maybe they'll go away," I whispered in her ear and nibbled on the lobe.

Stevie gasped and wrapped an arm around my neck, threading her fingers through my hair and tugging harder than I expected. "Or maybe, if we're really loud, they'll go away." To punctuate her point, she reached between us and pressed me against her opening.

A loud, continuous knock sounded on the cottage's front door and we both groaned. "Guess not."

"I'll go talk to them." She fell against the bed and let out a long sigh, but I couldn't look away from the beautiful jiggle of her breasts. "In a minute."

"No, stay here," I whispered and leaned forward, pulling her nipple into my mouth and rolling it around between my lips and tongue. The knocking sounded again, louder this time.

"If I stay any longer, we'll be putting on a show. For your grandmother."

I rolled off her easily. "Fine. Hurry back." I reached out and smacked her ass just before she was out of reach, and my gaze stayed glued to it until she covered it up with a silky kimono-style robe.

When Stevie was gone, I fell back on the bed and stared up at the ceiling, wondering what in the hell I was doing. Having fun was the first answer that came to mind, but even I knew it was more than that. I wouldn't mess around with an employee for a few nights between the sheets. Nothing could come of this, not really. Stevie and I were too different, despite the fact that we couldn't seem to stay away from each other. Then again, maybe some good, hot fun was exactly what we both needed.

"We need your help," Eddy told Stevie, and I didn't have to see her to know she was trying to finagle her way inside.

"I'm listening," Stevie told her, doing her best to sound both tired and bored.

"Rafe needs to fly out to Denver for one of those fancy firefighter conferences," Janey explained.

"Sure wish they would open those things up to the public," Eddy mused, dirty old lady that she was.

"Anyway, it's just a quick overnight trip, and he needs someone to keep him organized. He's giving a keynote address and needs to attend several specific talks in order for the Feds to pay for the additional training."

None of this sounded on the up-and-up to me, but I wasn't here, which meant I didn't get an opinion. "Doesn't the fire chief have an assistant?"

"Of course he does, but poor Lydia isn't up to the task of running around a giant event venue, bless her heart. Can you do it?"

"The city will pay your airfare and hotel, plus meal stipends," Janey added, but no matter how much they sweetened the pot, I didn't like it. I knew exactly what they were up to and, dammit, I didn't like it one bit.

"I already have a job," she argued, instead of outright telling them no.

"If you can do Friday and Saturday, that's when most of it takes place. And, if things go well," Eddy added, letting the last word linger in the air long enough to make sure all of Texas got her point, "maybe you won't come home until Sunday afternoon."

"Eddy," she groaned. "Please."

"What? I'm just saying, it doesn't seem like things are working out with you and Scotty."

"Cut it out, old woman, and tell me what you're up to. And don't lie to me," she insisted in an impressive tone that, somehow, worked.

Eddy huffed, annoyed. "If Scotty's too stupid to see what's in front of him, maybe Rafe won't be. He's gorgeous with a great body—what's not to like?"

I shook my head, making a note to take my own grandmother off my holiday list after that little betrayal.

"So, you just want to throw me at another of your Hometown Heroes?" Stevie demanded. "No thanks."

I couldn't help but smile at her tone, even though I know it had very little, if anything, to do with me.

"Not throw, girl, sheesh. You young people are so dramatic. I heard you two had a good time over at the Black Thumb, and that's as good a place as any to start." I could just picture Eddy doing her best to look like an innocent old woman. It was her go-to move, but her mistake was using it in a town where everyone knew all of her tricks.

"You're right, he is gorgeous. And funny. And yeah, he's even charming. But he's not ready for anything at all, and I'm not interested in anything more than friendship with him."

"You sure?"

"I am," Stevie answered, amusement lacing her tone.

"Dammit. Well, then, I guess Elizabeth can let Lydia go now."

"Wait a minute, you kidnapped her?"

"No," Eddy said, all righteous indignation. "We just waylaid her, is all."

Stevie let out another amused laugh and I wondered how she had adjusted to the craziness of Tulip so easily. "Sorry. Maybe Janey can go. She's young, organized, and able-bodied. And, if I'm not wrong, single, too."

I could only imagine the glare Janey was sending Stevie at the moment. "I'm busy."

"It's just a couple days," Stevie parroted back. "Three, if things go well."

"You haven't seen Scotty, have you?" Eddy's voice grew louder and I knew she was suspicious, but I had no way to alert Stevie.

"Yep. He's in my bed right now. We've been going at it like rabbits since last night. I was barely able to even walk to the door, but somehow, here I am." Her deadpan delivery was a dead giveaway, and Janey laughed.

"Well, I, for one, hope it's true. Give it to her good, boy!"

I cringed and covered my head with a pillow until the muffled sound of the door closing managed to break through. When the coast was clear, I found Stevie in the front half of the cottage, still staring at the door. "I can't believe you said that to her."

She was startled for a second before turning to me. "They deserved to hear that—and more."

"Like rabbits?"

She shrugged and stepped into my arms. "It was more of a goal than a description. When do you have to leave?"

Looking at the desire burning her violet eyes turned the fire inside of me all the way up and I scooped her in my arms. "Not until I'm done," I told her and carried her back to the bedroom, where we stayed until sometime late Sunday afternoon.

STEVIE

*A*nother work day was over. Instead of heading to my house or Scott's for another evening in front of the TV—at least, until we got naked and sweaty together—I was going home to change out of my work clothes, which were stained with ink and doggy slobber and enough animal hair to open a small pet salon. Because I was going out tonight. Well, *out* was kind of an understatement here in Tulip, but apparently Trivia Night at Black Thumb was a big deal, and Mikki had insisted I show up. The "or else" was implied.

Since Scott had left the office a couple hours ago to take care of a call he didn't need my help on, I decided to stop in and see what all the fuss was about. I wasn't exactly dressed to impress in simple jeans and a t-shirt, but I was happy to see casual was the attire of the day inside Black Thumb. Mikki and Bo sat at one of the groups of tables that had been arranged around a small elevated stage area, and I grabbed a pitcher of root beer from Buddy and joined them.

"Hey, girls. I got this round."

Mikki's eyes went round and then a few tears streamed down her cheek, which she fanned furiously. "Sorry. I mean, thank you. These pregnancy hormones are giving me whiplash."

"Me too," Bo grumbled and filled up three tall glasses. "But at least it was Stevie making you cry this time."

"Hey!"

Bo shrugged unapologetically and grinned. "Stick around a little while and then we'll talk."

Stick around a little while. It was the one thing I couldn't be counted on to do, which meant I shouldn't get too cozy with anyone in town. But one thought of Scott and my mind started thinking, *maybe you should.* "Are the mood swings that bad?"

Mikki smiled and wiped her eyes. "They just come out of nowhere. Buddy told me on the street yesterday that pregnancy agrees with me, and I cried for an hour. Watched a sad story on the news and bawled my eyes out. For thirty seconds." She shrugged like it was no big deal and chugged her soda. "It's an adjustment."

"But at least you'll have a cute little baby once this is all over."

"That's true." She smiled softly and rubbed her belly in gentle circles. "I can't wait to meet him or her."

"Hey, I heard you're good at organizing. How about you help me plan this one's baby shower?"

I frowned. "Isn't that kind of a personal thing to do?"

Something that friends or family members did for one another as a way to show their love and affection? I had missed all three of my sisters' baby showers.

"Not at all. In fact, this is the perfect way for you to get to know more people in town."

"Not sure I should. This job isn't guaranteed to last."

Mikki frowned. "But I thought you and Scott were an item."

As much as two people who were all wrong for each other could be, I supposed. "We are, but that's no more certain than the job." Both of them looked as if they wanted to say more but we weren't close enough for them to pry, which I appreciated—they seemed like the only two people in Tulip who didn't push.

Eventually, Trivia Night got underway, and I stopped watching the door and stopped wondering if Scott would show up by the fifth question. By the eighth question, I was full-on having a blast, shouting out answers along with three other women on my team.

"Okay, right now, the Chatterboxes are in the lead," Nina began with a teasing smile, "but the next round is double the points, so it's still anybody's game. Back in fifteen minutes." She sauntered off the stage and I used the time to escape to the silence of the bathroom.

My teammates were all nice, sweet, and smart women I'd love to be friends with if I stayed in town, but they were all *such* a part of each other's lives I wondered if it was even possible. Could I go from my solitary existence to a life filled with nosy, but well-meaning friends and neighbors? I didn't know but, suddenly, I kind of wanted to try. Though I had no clue how to even begin, I left the bathroom with a renewed sense of purpose. Maybe I could stay in Tulip, no matter what.

A broad-chested obstacle stood in my way with an enticing smile. "Fancy meeting you here." Scott had one hand braced on the wall beside my head and the other at my hip.

"Is it? Because I'm pretty sure I told you I'd be here tonight."

He shrugged, his smile so distracting I didn't notice him drawing closer, until not even air could pass between our bodies. "I must have forgotten." Then, his lips were attached to mine intimately, his tongue tracing the shape of my mouth before sliding across the seam, slow and tantalizing, until I moaned into his. Only then did Scott pull back with a satisfied smile. "Hey."

"Hey, yourself." My own words came out breathy, husky, and filled with carnal heat. This was what it felt like to crave someone, to just want to be near them because that one word made me feel like a giddy school-girl who was making out with her most secret crush.

"I just remembered," he said with a scratch of his chin, "that I forgot to feed Hershey." Scott did his best to look innocent as he said the words, but the corners of his mouth trembled with unspilled laughter.

My own lips curled into a smile. "That's mighty irre-sponsible of you, Dr. Henderson." Heat flared in his gaze at my words and he licked his lips.

"It really is," he agreed easily. "The problem is, I've had a beer or two and I need a ride." He let the words linger in the air between us as his thumb brushed back and forth along the soft skin at the waistband of my jeans. "Think you can give me a ride home, Stevie?"

Scott was toying with me, and worse, it was working. His words combined with his nearness, his scent, and the way his rough hands felt on my skin was unbelievably effective. I was a hot and bothered, horny mess of woman. "I suppose that could be arranged." It took me all of two minutes to get back to the table, make my excuses to the girls, and slide behind the steering wheel to take us home.

"You can stop here." Scott's voice was gentle, but that rope of sexual tension was still tight as could be.

I stopped the car and jumped out. Ever since we'd started whatever this was what we were doing together, we always went to my place. I never thought anything of it until this moment, and until that look in his eyes.

Something was different.

"Come on." With an easy smile, Scott grabbed my hand in his and pulled me inside a house that would be best described as a mansion. It wasn't just big, it was spacious, with plenty of moonlight filtering in through the over-sized windows. "Want the ten-cent tour, first?"

"Make it a quarter and you've got yourself a deal." I could admit to a certain amount of curiosity about Scott's house. Was he a neat freak or a secret slob? Did he sleep in the middle of his bed, or reserved a side for his future partner?

The answers came easy. Scott's living space reflected the same simple, easy-going personality as the man himself. The living room was exactly what you'd expect of a bachelor, only super high-end because he was a doctor *and* a bachelor. The sofa was huge, and the real leather was as soft and buttery as it came. A big-screen television was the center of the room, complete with large speakers and a smartphone dock below, which was probably a nice add-on to the gaming consoles taking up room on a shelf below.

The formal dining room was sparsely decorated and obviously rarely used. "Unless my parents are in town and insist on family dinners."

"Does that happen often?"

"Thankfully, no. They didn't make time for us when we were young and could have used them, and now that goes double, maybe triple." There was so much wrapped up in that short statement that I had the feeling Scott and I had more in common than either of us realized.

"One less room to clean," I told him, in hopes of erasing those shadows from his eyes.

"Exactly." We climbed the stairs after he showed off his home gym and I laid eyes on two more guest rooms, each barely decorated but with very specific color themes. "And this is the bedroom."

It was simple and beautiful, just like him. Dark blue and green dominated with cherry wood furniture that gave everything a masculine feel that only made me feel more feminine. Somehow.

"Very nice."

Scott raised our clasped hands to his mouth and pressed a kiss to the back of my hand, shocking the hell out of me. "Glad you approve, because I'm hoping that's where we end up." The heat in his eyes left no mistaking what he wanted.

"Why wait?" I stepped in closer, ready to take exactly what my body had been begging for since he found me at the bar, but Scott took a step back.

"Because I need fuel." With a short, sharp kiss to my lips, he turned around and tugged me out of the bedroom and back down the steps, saving the best room for last. "And this is the kitchen."

It was nice, the same cherry wood that didn't shrink the cavernous room but gave it a high-end gloss that was breathtaking. The black granite counters had the thinnest thread of silver woven through them, creating a stunning liquid look. "Wow. This looks like a room where a lot of cooking takes place."

"Sometimes, the housekeeper leaves meals for me, otherwise it's wasted on me. Much to Eddy's great disappointment."

I flashed a distracted smile, my gaze focused on the mountain of food on the smaller table for four nestled beside French doors that opened onto a small terrace. "Planned all this, did you?"

A slow smile spread across Scott's face, his green eyes sparkling like emeralds that had been blended with jade to create a whole new gem. He nodded slowly and pulled me into his arms, wrapping those big muscles around my waist. I sank into his embrace. Relaxed into it, even, closing my eyes and taking in the way he felt and smelled this close. "I didn't want to share you today. Is that bad?"

Hell no, it was incredible. "I guess that depends on what you plan to do with me."

He smiled and kissed one side of my neck and then the other. "I was thinking that, first, I would feed you." He kissed the pulse racing at the base of my throat and motioned toward the food on the table. "Then, I was thinking maybe you could feed me." Before I could see the dark intent in Scott's eyes, his mouth was on my neck again, driving me wild to make sure he got exactly what he wanted.

Scott was insatiable and I loved that about him. Not just because it made me feel like the most desirable woman in the whole galaxy, but because it made me *feel* things I thought I was no longer capable of feeling. Crazy. Out of control. Unhinged by desire. I cupped his face, my gaze serious as I made the internal decision to throw myself wholeheartedly into this thing with Scott, and I licked my lips. "I'm down with that plan."

"Excellent." That one word revealed his relief, which made me feel better about the recklessness of going all in with this particular man. "Have a seat and I'll grab some dishes."

"Was there even an emergency this afternoon?" I asked, and he flashed a look that told me it was all a ruse. I frowned. "But, why?"

"I wanted to surprise you."

"Well, you did." I hadn't expected anything like this of Scott, not because I didn't think he was capable but, honestly, I didn't think I mattered enough to him.

"Good surprise?"

I scanned the table and all the delicious, greasy food laid out just for me. Mini pizza bites, spicy chicken chunks, sweet potato fries, bacon mac & cheese, steak strips, and taco fixings. "The best surprise."

He blinked, shocked at my effusive words. "Then it was all worth it."

So far, I had to agree. "Did you cook all this yourself?"

"With a lot of help, yes. I think my housekeeper is working for Eddy, because when she found out it was for a woman, she suddenly became very eager to help."

I shook my head. "This town really is unbelievable."

"I know," he agreed with an affectionate smile as he brought the dishes to the table. "Still, I prefer to keep this kind of business between us." I froze at the too-familiar words that brought me back to my first year on my own, and the much older doctor I'd been dating who'd wanted to keep us a secret. "Only because I want this to work, or not work, because of us. Not outside pressure or expectations."

"Okay, that's fair," I admitted and he smiled before leaning in to press a slow, drugging kiss to my mouth.

"Glad you agree." His gaze lingered even as he sat back and casually stacked his plate with a little bit of everything. "Do you miss farm life?"

"Uh, no, not particularly. I loved growing up on farms, but I'm not sure it was the life for me."

"What about your family in Australia?"

"That's not my family. That's my father's family—he is our only connection, which is barely a connection to me." I wasn't bitter, not anymore. It was what it was.

"You're hurt."

I shrugged. "Even if I am, what difference would it make? That wouldn't change anything that happened." And I had wasted enough of my life wishing the past was different.

"Is that why you already have one foot out the door?"

I wanted to be mad at Scott for calling me out like that, but he was right. "Probably." I shrugged. "I think I inherited the wandering gene from my dad."

"Maybe," he said thoughtfully and I sat up straighter, recognizing the signs that he had something on his mind. "Have you ever thought about staying in one place?"

"Of course I have. Plenty of times."

"But?"

I shrugged off the question, feeling suddenly uncomfortable. "But in the end, I didn't stay."

"Why?"

"A variety of reasons. The job ended, a relationship ended, or it was just time to move on." There was never anything or anyone compelling enough to make me stay. Instead of revealing that, or worse—the fact that Scott might just be compelling enough to make me stay—I smiled and changed the subject. "Do you miss the NFL?"

He shrugged. "Some days I do, especially during football season. The game itself is amazing and some days I think I must have been crazy to let it all go, but nothing beats sunsets, wide open spaces, and blueberry wine." His gaze lingered on mine, his eyes telling me more than his mouth would allow. "And, of course, the company."

I pushed back my plate of half-eaten food, determined

to return to it later, and raised my glass in the air. "Who can pass up blueberry wine and damn good company?"

With a surprised smile, Scott raised his own glass in the air. "Indeed." We both took slow sips of the delicious but potent wine, our gazes locked in a dark, intense stare-off that sent heat pulsing through my veins.

"Dinner was delicious, Scott. Thank you."

"It was my absolute pleasure, Stevie. I assure you."

I believed it, and knew it was time to return the favor. "In that case, isn't it about time that I make sure you get fed?" Heat instantly lit his gaze and he stood, pushing his chair back until it tipped over. In the next moment, Scott was in front of me, lifting me in his arms and kissing the hell out of me.

I didn't resist. Instead, I melted into him like butter.

SCOTT

"*S*cott. Just the man I wanted to see." Janey's voice brought me up short and instantly, I regretted leaving my office. The plan had been to come up front and get a little handsy with Stevie, since we were between appointments, but now it looked like Hometown Heroes duty would rear its ugly head once again.

"What's up, Janey?" I did my best to keep the whine out of my voice because the truth was that I was happy to help, honored, in fact. But when I had agreed to the calendar, I was under the mistaken impression that would be it, but then it had turned into town activities and community service. Now, it was just this whole *thing*.

"You guys might start making me believe you're not happy to see me," she said on a fake pout as she shared a conspiratorial glance with Stevie. "Anyway, I'm here because picture time has arrived."

"Great," I deadpanned, making both women laugh.

"I know, how terrible it must be that a whole town

thinks you're hot enough to buy a photo of you, and it's for charity. Ugh, that sounds awful," Stevie added, not bothering to skimp on the sarcasm. When I glared, she held her hands up defensively and mimicked zipping her lips.

"Better," I growled, barely resisting the urge to leap over the reception desk and ravish her. I turned to Janey. "Just tell me when and where." I would do my part, but I didn't have time for any more than that.

Janey smiled at Stevie again, one brow arched in skepticism. "You have to tell me your trick, Stevie. Maybe I can use it on the rest of the Hometown Heroes to get my way." They laughed again, but I was focused on what 'trick' Stevie was using on me. "I haven't come up with a concept for you yet, Scotty boy. So, you have some more time, I just wanted you to know you were next up."

Lucky me. Every other hero had told horror stories of Janey forcing them to talk about their feelings or trying to talk them into shirtless photos, and several had stories of the older women in town, like Eddy, showing up to ogle them during the photo sessions. None of that sounded all that appealing to me. "Thanks."

"Why don't you just shoot him at his house with Hershey? The dog is damn adorable, and since he'll never go shirtless, this is as hot as you're probably gonna get."

Janey stared at me with her head tilted—her thinking position, as I called it—and I braced myself for whatever burst of genius she was about to unleash. "How about no shirt *but* with a lab coat?"

I appreciated her determination.

"No."

"Plus a stethoscope?"

"Still no, Janey."

She gave her best pout but it had no effect on me. I'd known her too long. "Fine. I'll be by this week to check out your property again, and I'm shooting for next Friday."

"Sounds good," I told her, even though it sounded like the last thing I wanted to do.

"I hope so, because we're down to the wire and I still have more concepts to create. This Hometown Heroes calendar is taking over my whole life," she grumbled.

"Serves you right for coming up with this idea," I told her unsympathetically.

"It'll be excellent for your portfolio," Stevie told her with a smile. "And you could probably become mayor after all this, if you wanted."

Janey laughed. "Wouldn't Leland just get a kick out of that?" She shook her head. "Please don't mention that to him. Either of you." She pointed at Stevie and then me, but I only smiled with a small shrug.

"No promises."

With a frustrated groan and a promise to see me soon, or maybe it was a threat, Janey walked out of the office, finally giving me some alone time with Stevie.

"You enjoyed that," I accused when she was gone.

"Maybe just a little." Stevie smiled, her thumb and forefinger less than an inch apart. "The whole thing is fascinating, you have to admit—hot do-gooders for charity. It's genius, and I've already preordered my copy."

My brows arched and I closed the distance between us, gripping the circular desk so Stevie was trapped by my arms. "You get to see all this whenever you want and still, it's not enough?"

"Never said it wasn't enough, just that a calendar includes eleven other hotties and I like man candy as much as the next woman." Her gaze heated. "I suppose, though, there is something to be said for live, in-your-face man candy."

I didn't miss the heat or the intent in her gaze, and when she took a step back, I grinned. "Where are you going, Stevie?"

"Nowhere," she said, and took another step back. Then another, and another, until she was halfway down the hall.

When she took off, my feet were on the move, following her into the supply closet. "A little cramped for my tastes, but I like it."

She turned with an admonishing finger. "Work, Dr. Henderson. It's time to work."

"Oh, I plan to put in some work. Some very *hard* work," I said, making her laugh.

"Cheesy," she accused with a laugh and I took my moment, fusing our mouths together in a long, hot kiss that would have steamed up all the windows if the supply closet had them. Her lips and her tongue mingled with mine and something happened. I couldn't possibly explain it, other than to say it felt like it was a lot more than fun. It was absolutely fun and exhilarating, but it had turned into something more.

"You like cheesy," I growled and pulled her in for just

one more taste. My hands fisted in her thick black locks, fingers twirling around the heavy waves to pull her closer, to get more of her. For a better taste.

Just one more taste.

One more taste turned into two, and then into three before we were interrupted by the sound of the next appointment arriving.

Luckily, we had plenty of time to pick up where we'd left off later.

STEVIE

*P*icking up lunch for Scott while I was out on my own lunch break had become kind of a habit—and one I wasn't all that comfortable with, thanks to a past relationship. But the man worked hard and he refused to even consider adding another doctor to his practice until he'd repaid Eddy and started operating fully in the black, something that could happen sooner rather than later if he wasn't so damn stubborn.

"Hey, Stevie!" Ginger's smoky voice sounded across the diner, her wide smile always a welcome sight. "Your order will be up in a minute. Want some coffee?"

I shook my head. "If I have any more coffee today, my heart will explode." She laughed, and I joined in with her. "But tea sounds good. Earl Grey, please."

"Coming right up!" Ginger bounced from table to table wearing a wide smile that might make some customers think her shift had just started when the truth was, I saw her almost every morning on my way to the clinic. She took the morning shift at Big Mama's and then headed over to the newspaper office for the rest of the day. She worked hard and had somehow made a life for herself, though no one knew her story, which kind of reminded me of… myself.

Tulip was such a good place, a nice place, the kind of place a certain type of city folk moved to so they could raise a family and live a simpler life. I didn't belong in this town any more than I belonged anywhere else, especially with Scott, but somehow, both had wrapped tightly around my heart. Somehow, this place and this man had me floating instead of walking, humming and smiling instead of scowling and complaining. I wasn't just happy, I was satisfied. And constantly aroused.

And it was all Scott's fault. "Here ya go." Ginger dropped off the bags and took my cash before flashing a hurried smile and dashing off once again.

My thoughts returned to Scott and this damn postcard of a town. Last night, I hadn't been able to sleep, even though my body was exhausted and wrapped in Scott's arms. I'd realized that this was the first time since my mom died that I'd actively reached out and tried to be happy. There was something about this place that allowed you to *just be* happy without a lot of effort, it was so organic you hardly realized it was happening until you were one of those people who stopped in the middle of the sidewalk to hold a full conversation with a random person.

Instead of yelling at them for screwing up the flow of traffic, I was now that person. Even though, now, I was *reluctantly* that person. "Elizabeth. Eddy. Fancy running into you ladies." Not really, since I knew they saw me go into Big Mama's and had then maneuvered themselves into my path before I reached the office.

"Seems like you plan on sticking around, after all." Eddy folded her arms and tried hard for a scowl, but it never materialized.

Here we go. "I'm not sure," I told her honestly, refusing to tell the old lady what she wanted to hear simply because I was sleeping with her grandson. The truth was that Scott didn't need me, didn't need a full-time assistant at all now that everything was all caught up.

"That's too bad," Elizabeth said ominously, sending the tiny hairs on my body standing in an upright position. "Well, Mayor Ashford has an opportunity to discuss with you when you have time. If I were you, I'd make it a priority," she added with a pat on my shoulder before both women walked away.

I stared after them for a long time, wondering what in the hell they were up to now, because news of my temporary stay in town didn't seem to leave as much impact as it had a month ago. Two months ago, even. "What the hell is wrong with me?" Was I now upset that the matchmaking old ladies had given up?

A little bit, yeah.

But that was crazy, so I shook the thought off and made a note to figure out how I could get in to see the mayor of Tulip. How did one even go about setting that up? I wasn't a meet-the-mayor kind of girl and therefore, totally out of my element. But I was always on the lookout for my next opportunity, and this could very well be it.

After I finished my work today, anyway. My feet were back on the move, carrying me and lunch back to the quiet office where Hershey and the pony were our only animal visitors. Usually, there were a few animals that spent a night or two, but this week we were blessedly empty, which was why it felt so quiet when I walked through the front door.

Almost too quiet, since I'd gotten use to the chaos of working with Scott. A veterinarian's office was about as calm and quiet as a pediatrician's, so to find the lobby area empty and completely silent in the middle of a weekday was kind of disconcerting. I shook off that thought, chalking it up to the fact that I'd let the matchmakers get in my head, and walked to my desk. I set down the bag containing my nacho fries and shook off my jacket, hanging it on coat rack in the corner. I took a moment to organize and straighten the piles of magazines it seemed that Scott never tossed away before the next round of appointments started to arrive, a half an hour from now.

A quick scan showed the front of the office was set to rights, which meant I could drop off Scott's lunch and have my own in peace before things got crazy again. The office still seemed too quiet, especially since I knew Scott was probably still hunched over his laptop, working, and my steps turned careful. It wouldn't be the first time I found a tweaker inside a doctor's office, but this time I would be prepared.

If I needed to be.

A quick knock and then I pushed open his door, ready to see Scott's bent head or a shaky addict looking to score. What I saw when I stepped inside shocked the hell out of me. Clara was there, and she was standing close enough to Scott that I'd bet he could tell whether that small strip of red peeking out the top of her shirt was, in fact, lace or silk. Whatever they were talking about, it was serious. And intimate.

"I brought you lunch." It was the most asinine thing I could have said in the moment, I knew that, but this was my job and I couldn't risk it for anything.

Or anyone. Not even my own stupid heart.

Before Scott could say anything, I darted from his office, ignoring the triumphant look on Clara's face that I didn't buy for one damn minute. I knew her type, had known girls and women like her my entire life, and I had never let them get to me. Not even now, because I knew her game.

That wasn't what bothered me when I yanked my bag off the desk and marched into the seldom used break room to enjoy my damn nacho fries. No, it wasn't that I thought that Scott had *somehow* found time in his busy schedule to screw around on me. Nope, I was more worried about my response in that breath of a moment, when I'd thought maybe there was something going on between them. In that flash of a second, my heart broke. It ached, like someone had torn it straight down the middle with their bare hands, and that was *not* the response of a woman having a good time, just enjoying some casual sex with a very gorgeous man.

That was the response of a woman who didn't just *want* more, but she was expecting more, and that was just stupid. It was especially stupid since I was that woman and I knew there was no future with me and Scott. He would eventually marry a woman like Clara—maybe not as ice cold and shallow, but a woman as sophisticated and put together as he was. He wouldn't go for a career assistant with no family to speak of, because that wasn't appropriate. And Scott was only inappropriate in the bedroom.

The thought produced a shiver straight down my spine that I was determined to ignore. None of this was good news, not one damn bit of it. I couldn't start having *serious* feelings for Scott. He was my boss—my very temporary boss, but still—and he was all wrong for me. As wrong as I was for him, which meant it was a thought I needed to put away where I kept other things I didn't have time or energy to think about.

"You're upset." Scott's deep voice tore through my racing thoughts, startling me, and I glared up at him.

"I'm not upset." But if he asked that question more than once, there was a good chance I would be—and soon. I mean, I *was* upset, but not for the reasons he thought, because men were clueless. "What's up, Scott?"

"There's nothing going on with me and Clara."

I believed him and didn't need to hear the words, but since he felt compelled to say them, I took in the details. The lack of lines and creases on his face, the calm way he delivered the words with just enough annoyance to let me know he was offended I'd thought so. Even though I hadn't thought a damn thing.

Other than for that briefest of moments.

"I didn't think there was," I told him honestly, nearly bursting out laughing at the scowl he sent my way.

Confused, Scott folded his arms over his massive chest, showing off sun-kissed skin and arm hair that was practically blond from exposure. "Then why are you mad?"

I was mad because this thing between us was supposed to be fun. Really hot and temporary fun, and now that I knew it had moved well beyond *just fun* and into something else, I couldn't ignore it. But I didn't say any of that. "You said I was mad, not me."

Scott sighed, trying hard to rein in his temper. "You're acting mad, Stevie. I'm not making this up."

"Am not." Yep, it was the height of childish arguing, and it was all I had.

"You're doing a damn good impression of a pissed off woman, then." He sat down, but instead of choosing the chair across from me like a normal human being, he dropped down into the chair right beside me and faced me, pulling me and my chair between his thighs so we were close. Legs touching and breaths mingling, we stared at each other for a long, breathless moment.

"Maybe I have just have a resting bitch face." My chin tilted up in defiance, daring him to call me out on my lie, but this was Scott and he wasn't at all moved by my tough-girl act.

He laughed and shook his head. "Or maybe, you're

bothered by the thought of me with another woman. That's okay, Stevie, I like seeing you a little jealous."

I barked out the fakest laugh in my arsenal. "Jealous? Why would I be jealous when a woman like Clara is exactly who you'll end up with?" I was still ignoring the pang that had returned to my general chest area.

"Bullshit," he spat the word angrily and cupped my face. "I already told you I wasn't interested in Clara," he said, turning me to face him no matter how much I squirmed to avoid looking directly into that green gaze. "Something is going on, with you and between us, and we both know it. I can get it out of you now, if you like." Scott leaned forward until his lips were on the delicate skin of my neck, up to my chin and then my mouth for a hot but too-short kiss. "Or I can take my time and get it out of you later."

"Later's good." Later allowed me at least a few hours to get my head screwed on right, so I could enjoy another night in bed with Scott. Later gave me plenty of time to take these mixed-up emotions and ball them up and shove them deep down into a box that would be taped, locked, and sealed with a fingerprint scan, never to be opened again.

Then I would be free to just *enjoy* the simple pleasure of being with Scott for as long as it lasted.

"Then later it is," he whispered in my ear, letting out a deep chuckle when his words produced a shiver.

"Good." I stood and straightened my super casual office attire of jeans and a T-shirt. "Great. Perfect."

"Excellent," he added, amusement coloring his tone.

"Superb," I shot back and pushed away from him and the table, standing so I could get some fresh air before the next round of people and animals arrived.

"Stevie?"

I stopped inside the doorway and turned to Scott's handsome face and full-watt smile. "Yeah?"

He stood and bridged the gap between us, looking me right in the eyes with a gravely serious expression. "I really can't wait until later."

My lips curled into a reluctant smile as I revealed my own truth. "Me either, Scott." Me either, damn you.

SCOTT

"*W*hen you said later, I thought there would be more nudity involved." Stevie's grumbled words did nothing to ruin my good mood. She'd shown up and she'd made an effort, so the frustrated way she stabbed at the pile of buttery mashed potatoes on her plate and shoved them in her mouth with an erotic groan only made my smile widen. "Great food. Seriously lacking on the nudity, though."

Her complaint teased a laugh out of me and I shook my head, wondering if I'd ever had so much fun with a woman before taking her to bed. "I'll make it up to you, I promise."

It was a promise I couldn't wait to fulfill—hell, I'd spent the better part of the afternoon daydreaming, fantasizing about all the ways I would make her scream. Moan. Cry. And, most of all, to make her forget whatever she *thought* she had seen in my office earlier today. Though it had been nice to see that flash of jealousy and to think it was genuine, and about me. "But first, we have more planned before we go home."

Home. That word felt more like Stevie than the four walls of my house, the property that surrounded it, and even the town it was located in. Between her and Hershey, my house hadn't been so full and so noisy in... ever.

"More food?" Her violet eyes practically bugged out of her head and her hand immediately went to her stomach. "Any more food and the only thing we'll be doing tonight is falling asleep on the sofa like a couple of old folks."

I laughed again and shook my head, ignoring the warmth that spread through me at her words. It should have been more concerning to me that curling up on the sofa with this woman didn't sound so bad—in fact, it sounded pretty damn incredible. But Stevie wasn't ready to hear that yet. "I might be willing to risk it just to watch you eat some more."

Stevie arched a brow playfully. "Licking barbecue sauce off my fingers like an animal does it for you? Good to know." To make her point, she leaned in and slipped the tip of her thumb into her mouth, giving a pronounced suck before she pulled it back with a satisfied grin. A teasing grin. "Interesting."

"It does do it for me, Stevie. In a big damn way. In fact, I'm thinking of picking up a bottle before we leave. For later." I didn't miss the flare of heat in her gaze or the way her pink tongue reached out to wet her lips.

Stevie shook the moment of connection, of sexual tension, off with a smile. "I'm glad you didn't choose some fancy place. This food is really good, and there's more than enough of it."

A proud smile spread across my face at her words. All day, I'd gone back and forth between Reese's BBQ and one of the nice places on the edge of town, but Stevie was a simple girl who appreciated simple yet complex flavors. Like me, I think. "Then eat up, we've got plenty of time to work off some calories before we head home."

There was answering heat in her eyes, but more importantly there was a flush every time I said *home*, and I had a sneaky suspicion that meant even more to her. "Work off calories, you say?" Her attempt at innocence pulled another laugh from me and when Stevie excused herself to the bathroom, I took care of the bill *and* bought a bottle of Reese's branded sauce, just to get a rise out of Stevie.

When she returned to the table, I stood and wondered how in the hell we'd gotten here. How had this petite woman with so much attitude come to mean so much to me? What was it about Stevie that had captured my attention, when no one had in ages? "Are we gonna use that here, or are we heading out?"

Stevie stood beside the table with a sweater wrapped around her shoulders, blocking her tattoos from sight, and I blinked. "I'm not opposed to using it here, but Reese might have something to say about it."

Her lips twitched and she shook her head, amused and blushing as she headed towards the exit. "So, where to next, captain?"

"Captain?"

She nodded. "You're in charge here. For now," she added on a rushed breath. "For now."

'For now' was all I needed to get to the next step. Now that I was absolutely certain about what I wanted, there was no reason to delay or hesitate. Stevie was right here, primed, and all I had to do was play my cards right. "I can handle *for now*, Stevie," I told her as I helped her into the car and buckled her seatbelt. "There. All safe."

"Th-th-thanks," she stuttered and I pressed a soft, slow kiss right on those perfect lips before stepping back and closing the door. By the time I got settled behind the wheel, I had my body mostly under control. "So, where are we headed?"

"Someplace guaranteed to get your heart rate pumping and put a smile on your face."

She looked across the car at me with a sultry grin. "Promises, promises."

Was it too late to turn back around and head straight to my place? It wasn't, and the heat in her eyes told me she wouldn't be opposed, but that was for later. I had a plan and next, after food, was fun. Get Stevie good and relaxed before I took my moment.

"You surprise me, Scotty." Stevie looked up at me after three grueling games of air hockey. "This doesn't seem like your kind of place, and you've been a good sport so far."

I huffed out a laugh and wrapped an arm around her. "You're only saying that because you wiped the floor with me." Another thing I'd learned about Stevie was that she had a wicked competitive streak. "I think we ought to play darts next, or something that plays to my strengths."

"Because you're tall?" When I nodded, she let out a loud laugh that drew the attention of several other couples. "Let's see about that, then!"

For the next few hours we bounced from game to game, competing like there was some big prize to be won aside from bundles of tickets and oversized, overstuffed animals. "I think it's safe to say that darts is *my* game."

One look at my smug smile and Stevie shook her head. "I'll give it to you, but only because you were a good sport about losing skee-ball. And pool. And Pac-Man. What shall I beat you in next?" With an over-the-top stroking of her shin, Stevie looked around the vast entertainment complex and sighed. "Basketball?"

I didn't know if she was taking pity on me or what, but I appreciated the softness in her eyes and the way her hand grabbed onto my bicep. And I really appreciated the way her breasts pressed against my arm and she leaned against me as we made our way to the row of basketball hoops. "I guess we're gonna shoot some hoops. Unless you're a ringer?"

The laugh she sent my way was enough to send any red-blooded man to the emergency room—and I was a professional, I knew all the signs. Shortness of breath. Elevated pulse. Dizziness. Numb and tingling fingers. A complete and total lack of control. I had it bad. "Not a ringer, no. But I do all right. Scared?"

"Terrified," I admitted.

"Don't worry, Scotty." She gave my chest a sympathetic pat and I laid my hand over hers, letting her feel the rapid pace of my heart under her fingertips. "I'll go easy on you."

I would have loved nothing more than to say I bested Stevie at basketball, but the woman was formidable and she didn't like to lose. And worse, she didn't give up. "Was that taking it easy on me?"

Stevie looked at me, then at her scoreboard and then mine, and back to me. "Apparently it was, since you beat me by two hundred points." She sounded upset, but the glowing smile on her face suggested otherwise. "Good job."

"Thanks."

"I should thank you, this was an excellent date. Probably one of the best I ever had. So, thanks." Stevie seemed uncharacteristically shy in that moment as she pushed up on her tiptoes and pressed her soft lips to mine. The kiss was sweet, almost gentle and shy as her lips touched mine in caresses that grew in intensity with every pass of her tongue. The kiss quickly heated up and her soon her fingers sifted through my hair as my hands gripped her hips. The kiss threatened to explode right there in front of the row of basketball hoops and digital displays.

I pulled back with wide eyes and a thumping heart, surprised again by my reaction to this woman. "Well."

"Right?" She let out a nervous laugh and went in for another kiss that sent my senses reeling, and my knees damn near buckled in the middle of the gaming complex. "Yeah, wow is right."

Damn this woman and her incredible words. "Thanks," I told her with an amused laugh and clasped our hands together as I led her out to the car so we could go home where I could really show her just how much she meant to me.

"**I**s this the part where you kiss me good night and send me on my way?" It felt like my heart had been replaced by an entire marching band, beating loud, fast, and erratically as I stood in the middle of Scott's bedroom. Naked. Teasing him.

I couldn't deny that the way he looked at me in that moment, like I was the best damn thing he'd ever seen, was… intoxicating. It was thrilling. Just the look of desire in his eyes made me feel like the sexiest woman alive.

"Do I look like an idiot to you?" His lips kicked up to one side in a teasing grin, one brow arched in question.

"Well, with your mouth hanging open like that," I began and let the rest of that thought linger between us. Unspoken.

Scott's laugh came out rich and full-throated, the kind that startled you a bit before it became so contagious you couldn't fight it if you wanted to. And I definitely didn't want to. "You're standing in front of me wearing nothing but a scrap of purple that's being passed off as panties and a pair of high heels—how else should I be looking at you?"

Exactly like that. "For starters, I think you should be looking at me from a lot closer than this." Less than ten feet separated us, but it was still too far. My body pulsed with need for this particular man and now, with him just out of reach, it damn near vibrated. "Closer than that."

His grin spread and I felt it all throughout my body, warming down to the deepest parts of me as he stepped closer, his green eyes growing darker and darker the closer he came. One hand went to the curve of my waist, sliding up and down that crescent until I shivered, while the other speared through my hair and pulled me close. "Is this close enough?"

"It's a good start."

His mouth crashed down on mine, sweet and hot at the same time and I clung to his big shoulders as the kiss went on and on, deepening and changing several times before I had to come up for air. Unfortunately.

"A damn good start," I amended. He was so big and so wide, I tried to climb his big body.

"Glad you approve." His tone was amused and I smiled, happy to see the playful Scott show up tonight. Not just now, in the bedroom, but earlier for our date, too. I didn't expect he would be able to buck expectations and have a low-key date at a barbecue joint and a big ass arcade, but he'd jumped in with both feet and we'd both had a great time.

"I do," I told him with a sassy smile before he tossed me on the bed and crawled up after me. "But it was so long ago I've almost forgot—" His kiss cut off the rest of the words and it was just fine by me because he tasted like Dr. Pepper and chocolate and sugar, because he'd been unable to resist the funnel cake sundae. He devoured my mouth as quickly as he'd devoured the sundae, both times leaving me vibrating with need. And squirming in wet panties.

He pulled back and smiled down at me, green eyes dark and smiling, promising plenty of pleasure to come, and I felt my gut clench hard and my chest suddenly felt tight. Too tight. "Don't fight it." Scott whispered the words in my ear and then took his time making sure he pleasured every inch of my skin with his tongue. And I didn't fight it. In fact, I didn't just *not fight* it, I reveled in it. I closed my eyes and arched into him, licked my suddenly dry lips and tangled one hand in his hair until he was too far away to touch.

"Scott." As if I could forget who made me feel this way. This man who was smart and kind and funny even when he was being bossy and judgmental. This man who seemed amused when I brought out my bitch card and gave as good as he got, forgiving easily. Quickly. As if I could ever possibly forget this man who, I was pretty damn sure, I was in love with.

"I can't hear you." His words were muffled and when I looked down at him, those smiling green eyes were staring right back at me. Daring me. Teasing me.

He slipped two thick fingers inside of me at the same

time his lips closed around my clit and I was lost for I don't know how long as the orgasm worked its way to the surface in long, languid waves. Scott didn't let up, though, and continued to lavish that talented tongue on me until I couldn't tell if it was one orgasm or two. "Scott!"

His killer grin was my ultimate undoing. When he sat up and flashed a smile slick with my juices and there was something in his eyes that looked like more than lust, I lost it in a violent wave of erotic convulsions. "Fucking beautiful," I thought I heard him mutter but I was too lost to ecstasy to be sure.

I was trapped in my own thoughts and feelings, wondering if it was smart to keep going down this path. The itelligent thing would probably be to push him away and run off like a scared little maiden, embarrassed but with my heart intact. But Scott's lips worked their way up my body and I wasn't all that concerned with the smart thing.

Only the thing that felt good.

And Scott felt *damn* good. So good that I ached for him even as he slowly entered me, his gaze laser focused on mine so I couldn't look away. I could only stare at the play of colors in his eyes as his pleasure turned wild, the way his handsome features morphed into something dark and appealing when he was buried deep. "Stevie."

That was it, just my name. I smiled and wrapped my legs around his waist and decided that, for tonight, I would embrace this feeling. I wouldn't be terrified of it and I wouldn't run from it and try to put any distance between me and Scott, not while our bodies were tangled up like they were now. I embraced it, languished in pretending that this was more than the erotic event of my life as his hips worked in slow circles to drive me to the brink of insanity. I let myself believe it was love I saw shining in his eyes as he gripped my hips tight enough to bruise and pounded into me, harder and faster than I'd ever felt before. "Yes," I whispered, because my throat was too choked up with emotions to shout.

Scott changed his pace, keeping me guessing until my body simply took over, knowing instinctively what to do while my mind scrambled with unwanted emotions. "Fuck, Stevie!" His words came out on a harsh whisper as his tongue licked from my belly button all the way up to lips, his hips in constant motion as another orgasm welled up inside of me. "Yes!"

I didn't know if that was pride or satisfaction and I didn't care, at least I didn't think I cared. My body was nothing more than a mass of nerves, a bundle of feelings and they were firing on overdrive. As pleasure swamped my body, so did love and confusion and even a little bit of hate directed at yours truly. It was too much, but as every ounce of pleasure poured out of my body, I couldn't look away from the way Scott looked at me. It was real. It was genuine. It was... love.

It couldn't be, I knew that, but the hormones pumping through my body as orgasm number three or maybe number four overwhelmed me, it really felt like it. So, I did the only thing I could and slammed my eyes shut, allowing my body to absorb the memories of this night together.

Scott rolled us over so I was on top and I grinned. This would be the perfect way to remember this night, with me in control of his pleasure. I sat up straight and let out a long, low groan as my entire body pulsed with pleasure. "Oh, Scott!"

"Perfect," he growled and gripped my hips, his gaze focused exactly where it should be—on my boobs. Not my face. This way, I could watch him with his face twisted in raw desire as he chased down the pleasure I kept just out of reach. "Stevie," he growled, and it sent another shiver through me.

"Yes?" My hands went to Scott's massive chest and his green eyes were unavoidable as I began to slide up and down, faster and faster until his head fell back and his eyes closed a moment before his grip tightened.

"Oh, Stevie, oh fuck! Yes!" I went on and on, feeling another orgasm welling up inside me of me as Scott pumped his pleasure into my body. I felt like I was soaring, like actual euphoria was coursing through me, and I rode out the wave, risking another glance at Scott who smiled up at me as the last jerking convulsion tore through him.

Moments later, I collapsed on top of him, completely spent and unable to move. "That finish was even better than the start," I told him, making him laugh.

Scott pressed a kiss to the side of my forehead and held me until our bodies separated on their own, then he pulled me flush against his chest and wrapped those big, caring arms around me as my eyelids grew heavier and heavier. "Sweet dreams," he whispered. "Love you." The words were whispered so low as he kissed my shoulder that I wasn't sure I'd heard him correctly.

I was too orgasm drunk to say if it was dream or reality, but as I drifted off to sleep, I secretly hoped it was more than a hazy memory when the sun came up.

SCOTT

*T*he smells all around me in the kitchen were almost enough to distract me from the words that had been replaying in my mind since I'd woken up. An hour ago. *Sweet dreams. Love you.* My only defense, if I needed one, was that my defenses were down. Taking her, being with her the way we'd been together, it was an out-of-body experience. My mind and my body were as relaxed as they'd ever been in my adult life, and she was soft and smelled so fucking good, with that sexy satisfied smile on her face was everything.

It had all felt so right, Stevie in my arms after loving on her for so long, falling asleep before we woke up to do it all again. That little kiss on her shoulder, still damp from the exertion of our lovemaking, and uttering those soft words, had just fucking *felt* right. I wasn't sure if I owed her apology, but I damn sure hadn't planned on it, and she hadn't asked for one when she'd woken me up with her mouth in the middle of the night.

"Did you mean it?"

Shit!

I turned and found Stevie scowling at me, arms crossed over what looked like one of my old college t-shirts. It was too big and covered too much, but she looked good to me. "Good morning, Stevie."

"Morning," she grunted like it was a chore to perform even that one social nicety. "So… did you mean it?"

So, she wanted to dive right into it? Well, fine. I arched a brow and fought the grin tugging on my muscles. "Did I mean what?" I had to pull my lips into my mouth to stop the smile that was threatening to break free when her glare darkened and she pointed an accusing finger my way.

"You know damn well what I'm talking about, Scott."

I did, and I was glad in that moment that I wasn't smiling. This was serious business, and I'd never imagined I would be such an amateur to tell a woman I loved her for the first time while I was inside of her. Or when she was half asleep and unable to enjoy it.

She looked like a scared little kitten, trying to figure out if she should run or claw my eyes out, so I figured it was about time to stop messing with her.

"I do mean it. Have a seat."

"I'm fine," she insisted, notching her chin so high up in the air, I thought she might get carried away.

I turned a glare on her and growled, "Have a seat, Stevie." Stubborn damn woman was determined to drive me out of my damn mind.

She huffed out a breath before she dropped down in the nearest chair like it was some favor to me. There was already a plate of fruit on the table, along with sausage and bacon. "Well?"

"Hungry?" I knew she wanted to get right down to have *the conversation,* but she was too tense. I wanted her relaxed for this talk. Before she answered, I turned to the eggs just before they started to burn.

"I feel like I'm being screwed with, Scott, and I don't like it."

The vulnerability in her voice got to me and my shoulders sank. "I'm not trying to screw with you, but dammit, why are you so angry about this?"

She smacked her hands on the table and I turned to find a terrified, wide-eyed violet stare aimed at me. "Because I'm trying to figure out if that was post-orgasm bliss or reality!"

I nodded, sighing, and turned away. "I meant it."

"But you wish you didn't?" The hurt that mixed with hope in her voice was what strengthened my resolve. My determination.

"No, that's not it at all." I sucked in a deep breath and let it out for ten seconds before turning back to face her. She deserved to see my face and hear the sincerity in my words. "I wish I had chosen a better time to say it. It's not how I would have done it if I'd been thinking about it. But I meant it."

She still didn't seem completely convinced, and I took in another deep breath, knowing I would have to say the words again. "So, you didn't mean to say them to me? Out loud?"

I shook my head and dumped the eggs into a big bowl, which I brought to the table with more force than it required. For some reason, I'd decided to fall in love with the world's most skeptical woman. I stood in front of her, big and imposing because I knew she wouldn't be able to risk glaring up at me. "I didn't plan to say it when I did." That much was true.

"Okay."

"Stevie."

"What?"

"I love you."

Shock. That was the main expression on Stevie's face, which surprised me more than it should have, but there was also fear and hope, and that gave *me* hope.

"You love me." The words came out on a shaky breath.

When Stevie looked up at me, I nodded, expression serious so there was no misunderstanding my intentions.

"Are you sure?"

"I am."

"Okay, but how?"

I sighed and took the seat beside her, pulling her close. "I'm sure because I know myself. Because I've had other relationships and I didn't feel anywhere close to how I feel about you. Or when I think about losing you." That was what had convinced me if I was honest with myself.

"But how can you say that with such certainty? We're so different, you said so yourself."

"Yeah," I snorted. "A hundred years ago." At least, it felt

like she'd been part of my life for a lot longer than mere weeks.

"Sure, but you weren't totally wrong, either. I mean, this"—she waved back and forth between us, which I took as a good sign that she was already thinking of us as a couple—"could blow up in our faces."

"I know," I told her in mock seriousness. "We could even, *gasp*, end up married!" My words shocked her. Hell, I was waiting for my own shock to kick in, but it never did. I wasn't running for the hills and I wasn't even nervous at the idea of more.

"Don't joke about that."

"Who's joking?" She needed actual reassurance and I wanted to give it to her, so I grabbed her by the wrists and laid her palms over my chest. "I love you, Stevie, and I suspect that you love me, too. I know it shouldn't work, but it does, and I care more that I want you than I do that we might seem odd together."

"*Might* seem?" She let out an adorable unladylike snort that made me smile. "People will look at us and wonder when we'll flame out."

I smiled and leaned in. "Then I guess we'll just have to prove them wrong by *not* flaming out." But more than that, I didn't care. "If people can't look beyond your sense of style to see how amazing you are, how funny and witty, how sexy and smart, too, then they don't deserve to know you. Which works out for me, because I get you all to myself." The truth was that I wanted her to make friends, to settle into Tulip and have a life here.

With me.

"Scott." The word came out half plea and half whisper. "What if this is just hormones and newness and orgasms? I mean, we've had some incredible ones together."

"True." I could help but smile at her use of the word 'incredible.' "But those don't happen with everyone. Not like that." Stevie sighed and I tilted her chin up so those strange violet eyes were trained on me, so I could see the love she couldn't hide completely staring back at me. I held her close, my breath mingling with hers as we soaked each other in. "The fact that we shouldn't work but we do, and we want to, is a good thing. It means that we'll try harder to make this work. We won't let issues fester, we'll talk them out and we'll kick ass in this relationship. What do you think?" I held my breath, waiting for her walk away or smack me or laugh in my face. The way my heart was beating, all three were distinct possibilities.

"I think that you're crazy."

It wasn't a no. "I can work with that."

"I think you're crazy and I love you anyway, but we'll need more than that. I think so, don't you?"

She was scared that she would start to love me and love Tulip, and she would have to leave. I knew it and she'd hate it if I reminded her of that. "I think we got the bones of a solid relationship, Stevie. The fact that I love you helps a lot. So does the chemistry." Her cheeks pinkened and I grinned. "Care to share?"

"Nope," she said quickly and dipped her head, as if that could hide the blush staining her pale skin.

"Too bad." It didn't matter, not when I planned to give

her plenty of memories like that one from this point forward. I knew it with a certainty I hadn't had about anything since my decision to leave the NFL. That was why I wasn't haunted by it. "I love you and I promise not to hurt you on purpose. I don't have any more of a guarantee than that."

My words sank in and Stevie nodded. "Okay. Yeah. So… we're doing this."

"We are." I stood and pulled her flush against me, wrapping both arms around her waist so she couldn't get anyway. "I mean, I love you, and if you're sure you love me."

"I am," she said, quick enough that it made us both smile. "Last chance to back out, Scotty. After this, you're mine."

"I think I've been yours since you barged in and took over my office." On the surface, it was a ridiculous statement to make, given how angry I had been that day, but since she'd arrived my reactions to her had been anything but ordinary. "But since you don't seem sure, I guess I'll just have to show you how I feel." In fact, nothing sounded better than laying her out right here among all the other breakfast foods and feasting on her until she was sure.

"I was promised breakfast," she insisted with a phony pout and a lackluster shove at my chest. "It'll be here. When we're done. Sometime this afternoon."

Heat flared in her eyes at the promise and, because I loved her, I pretended not to notice the way she shivered. Or the way her nipples hardened. "I'll be cold by then."

"You'll be hungry, so it won't matter. Besides if you're really good, maybe I'll make it all over for you. Naked."

With a roll of her eyes and an overdramatic sigh, Stevie leaned into me. "You better live up to the hype, Dr. Henderson."

I wrapped my arms around her and reached for the hem of her t-shirt, tugging it up over her head and dropping it on the chair behind me. "Oh, I will. I promise."

She licked her lips, mesmerizing me while her hands made quick work of my boxer shorts. "I plan to make sure of it," she told me and pushed me down on the chair and straddled my hips. "I love you, Scott."

Perfect. It was the only word to describe how I felt in that moment. Hearing Stevie say those words felt right. It was like everything I never knew I wanted had just slotted into place and we came together hard and fast, exploding together in just minutes. "Love you too, Stevie."

She let out a laugh and reached for a slice of bacon, breaking it in half to share. "Good, because I don't think we should work together anymore."

I frowned, ready to argue, but maybe she had a point. Maybe she didn't. What mattered was that I wanted something else. "Fine, but you live here. With me."

"And Hershey?"

"Of course. We are a package deal."

Her smile brightened and she nodded. "Then I guess I'm moving in." Before I could let out a whoop of surprise, Stevie's arms were wrapped around me and her mouth was on mine, tempting me beyond reason as I hardened inside of her. It felt like we kissed for hours and hours, the perfect start to the rest of our lives.

The sound of the doorbell caused simultaneous growls to erupt out of us both. "If we're quiet, maybe they'll go away," I whispered.

"Scotty! Are you in there? Is Stevie in there with you?"

"Eddy," I mouthed to Stevie and she started to shake with laughter.

"Maybe we should be really loud and scare her off."

"No."

Stevie tightened and clenched around me and I couldn't suppress the groan. "Or, yes."

"Janey, do you see anything?"

At those words, I stood, our bodies still wrapped around each other's, and turned to the back door just in case Janey made an appearance. "We're being invaded."

She laughed. "Might as well answer the door. You do have your Hometown Heroes duties to tend to, and as the mayor's future executive assistant, I have to encourage this behavior."

It was the first I'd heard about the job with the mayor, but it meant she was sticking around. Growing her own roots. "I guess you have a point," I told her with a kiss. "But things were just getting good again."

"No kidding," she agreed on a throaty sigh and tightened around me again. "But the good news is we've got plenty of time to pick up where we left off. Later. Tomorrow. Next week. Next Month."

"Next year," I growled and kissed her again, slow and

hot until I wasn't sure I'd be able to open the door at all in the next hour. "Forever."

"Only time will tell," she said on a smile that told me she hoped as much as I did that time was kind to our love story.

~

The End

EXCERPT: COLD HEARTED LOVE

Sexy Small Town Sheriff Tyson was everything I shouldn't want in a man.

But I did.

It wasn't my fault I found the bossy lawman thing hot.

In my defence he kissed me first, I just…submitted.

We were all wrong for each other, but the thought of not seeing him again...

Impossible.

Somewhere along the way my enemy became something more.

He became my everything.

A reporter. Gorgeous. Stubborn. Mouthy.

Ginger was everything I didn't want in a woman.

Except she was fiery, and she didn't give up.

She kissed like her mouth was made just for me.

She had a way of making me forget she was a nosey journalist.

Always out for a story, no matter the cost.

Ginger made me laugh, she was a thorn in my side.

She made me fall for her.

But can I trust her with my heart when I don't know what she's hiding from me?

GINGER

One of the best things about having a hands off boss is that there was no constant presence hovering over you as you completed every single task assigned to you. One of the worst things, was when said boss never slept and communicated exclusively by email. Every single day. All day long. Some days I logged into the Tulip Gazette email system to find a dozen messages from the man who signed my direct deposit paychecks.

He was always respectful, mostly stern and usually redundant.

In conclusion Ginger, I am finding the Tulip Gazette a waste of resources. It turns a profit, but I feel it could b bigger. It should be bigger. Get those numbers up so we don't have to talk about things like shutting down the paper and unemployment claims. Greg T.

That's how he signed every message. Which didn't leave much of an impact on me, but the people of Tulip were utterly fascinated by him. His holiday cards and charitable donations have given him quite a reputation in Tulip, despite the fact he'd never set foot in this town. Ever.

Still, his message to me was crystal clear. Do better, or lose my job. Which basically meant, *do better,* because I couldn't lose my job. Decent paying positions were difficult to come across in this economy, and one with the flexibility to work another job was almost impossible. It's how I landed in this teensy town in the first place. The paper needed a journalist, and I was in need of a job in the field of journalism. It wasn't the best paying position, but now a few months later, I practically ran the place as a one woman operation for a slightly higher salary, which went to the pricey care home that treated my mom's Alzheimer's. It all worked out perfectly, because my part time job at Big Mama's diner paid my own living expenses. I *had* to stay on here.

No matter what.

I read Greg's email at least three more times, just in case the words shifted into something else that didn't threaten my employment status. Then I stared at the yellow notebook beside my tablet on the small wooden desk that counted as half of the Tulip Gazette offices. I had to come up with at least a hundred ideas if there was as chance in hell I found a dozen that could help drive more traffic, because more subscriptions were pretty much out of the question.

Tulip was a small town, I knew that when I packed up my apartment in Minneapolis, but that didn't bother me. It was certainly one of the smallest, with fewer than ten thousand people, but it wasn't my first small town. In my eagerness to earn more money, I hadn't stopped to figure out how I would keep up with the digital Joneses.

"I'll find a way." Mostly because I had to. It was just us, me and my mom. The Scanlan girls. She took care of me and put me through school, and now it was my turn the return the favor. Even if she had no idea what I was doing. Or for whom. That didn't matter, I wasn't doing it for the recognition or the gratitude, I was doing it for her.

Which meant I needed ideas. Lots and lots of ideas.

And I would come up with them. Soon.

For now, I had to get over to the diner before my shift began. The breakfast rush was crazy busy, and it was the best time of day to get good tips. Keep shift workers and retirees in steady cups of coffee and they were very generous before they headed off for another day of punching a clock. I had a few minutes before Big Mama expected me, so I took my time and enjoyed the scenery which included the infamous Tulip's Tribute, which is probably the sole reason the paper was still in operation.

"Morning Ginger." The sound of Rafe Montgomery's voice pulled me from my own thoughts and I smiled up at the too good looking fire chief.

"Good morning, Rafe. Fighting fires before the sun comes up?"

"Something like that," he grinned with twitching lips. "Breaking bad news to firefighters is best done with coffee and sugar."

"And don't forget carbs. Loads and loads of carbs." It

didn't do a thing to take the sting off bad news, but pastries were a special kind of miracle.

"Of course." His lips twitched again and I was never really sure if he was laughing at me or with me. "How are you settling into Tulip?"

"It's great," I told him honestly. "It's small and safe and weird as hell. What's not to like?"

"Maybe we ought to put that on the welcome sign. Welcome to Tulip. Where it's small, safe and weird as hell."

"Why not? We still have twelve hot hometown heroes to fall back on if that doesn't work." If possible, Rafe's cheeks turned an alarming shade of hot pink that teased a laugh out of me. "Sorry."

"Don't be. I should be used to it by now, but it's odd having your elementary art teacher ogling your ass."

"It'd be weirder if you were *still* in elementary art class." My words stopped him in his tracks, Rafe stared at me for a long moment and then he laughed. "Don't let it be weird, just flirt with her and move on."

"You don't know Mrs. Kendall."

I didn't, but the idea of another eighty year old with roaming hands was more entertaining than it had any right to be.

"Since you're already doing your part for charity, care to do a little more?"

He groaned and his broad shoulders fell. "How much of my precious free time is it gonna cost me?"

"Less than an hour, I promise!" His almost agreement had me feeling giddy as we neared the diner. "It's just a few paragraphs on fire safety during times of the year you think it's needed. Camping and hiking and skiing, all the activities that bring people here."

"That's a great idea. Count me in."

"Really? That's great Rafe, thanks!"

He held up his hand with a rueful smile. "Don't thank me yet, because I need you to remind me at least a week before you need it."

"Done!" I was so happy I practically vibrated with excitement. One agreement down, and it was just by accident. "Come on, let me buy you a cup of coffee and a sweet potato pecan muffin."

"Sounds like my lucky morning." He held the diner door open and I went in first, inhaling the scent of the first pot of coffee of the day and buttery biscuits already baking in the oven.

"Morning Big Mama!"

She grunted and flashed a beaming smile. "It is morning, ain't it? But that's not why you're smilin' so bright, is it?"

"No Ma'am it's not. Rafe has agreed to help me keep my job with some fire safety tips for the paper."

"He has, has he?" She wore a skeptical look and an arched brow. "Wonder what brought that on."

"I don't know, but I hope it means you'll agree to offer up some cooking tips to those not as capable as you are in the kitchen. No family secrets or anything, just how to properly coat chicken for frying, or the key to a moist cake. What do you think?"

"I guess it's my duty to pass my gifts on to the less fortunate."

"It would be what a good southern woman would do," I added because it was fun to banter back and forth with Big Mama.

"I knew I liked you for a reason." She pointed at me with a smile. "That coffee ain't gonna refill itself."

"No ma'am it won't," I shot back and strapped on a pink and yellow apron before grabbing a fresh pot of coffee and making the rounds as the diner filled up.

I spent most of the shift with a smile plastered on my face as I took orders, fed customers and cleaned tables. Pretty much I did whatever needed to be done to get the tables moving and new diners in their seats. But it was easy, I'd been waiting tables in one form or another since I was old enough to work. So what I spent my shift *really* doing was brainstorming. Thinking of all the ways I could recruit the townspeople to help drive traffic to the website and get them invested in it too, while making a list of who else I could ask.

By the time I untied the straps on my apron and left the diner for the Gazette offices, I felt a renewed sense of energy. A sense of hope.

I just hoped it worked out.

TYSON

"She's missing, Sheriff! My Marguerite is missing and I want her back!" Karl Gentry stood right outside the door of my cruiser with both hands flung high in the air and a wild look in his dark brown eyes. "Marguerite!"

I stepped from the cruiser slowly, giving myself plenty of time to stifle the laughter that threatened to build. Karl's pain was as real as any other citizen of Tulip, and I owed him my respect.

"Where did Marguerite get off to this time?" Every few weeks Marguerite, an eight hundred pound heifer, liked to go on a walkabout. Sometimes she was found lounging on another stretch of property, belly full with grass and a bovine grin on her face. Last year she managed to make it clear across town.

"Hell if I know, Sheriff. I woke up and she was gone. Just gone without a trace." Karl looked so bereft that I almost felt bad for the man, or I would if he ever bothered to repair his damn fence. "I'll bet, and you'll have to excuse me for sayin' so, but I'll bet it was your brother. He's always going on about how I treat my animals like he has any damn right…sorry, Sheriff."

"It's all right, Karl." I held up my hands to let him know I wasn't offended. Scott could be a little high and mighty when it came to his animals, it was a hazard of being a vet. "I doubt it was Scott, mostly because he doesn't have a place to keep your Marguerite."

"Then I don't understand where the hell she is, Sheriff!" The man was really flummoxed, and Marguerite was nowhere in sight, not in all four directions. "She's a damn cow, where could she be?"

It was a good question, but one I had no desire to debate over when lunch was close to an hour away, and my stomach was growling like a cave monster. "Let's give her some time to come home before we start to panic." I didn't bother telling him that a lost cow was no reason to call the Sheriff's Department, because I knew we'd still be back here again next month. Maybe sooner, if Marguerite got struck with cabin fever again.

Karl was getting ready to get himself worked up good and proper when we heard the telltale moo of his Marguerite. "You hear that?"

"Sounds like she just forgot to leave a note for you Karl."

His grin turned into a laugh and he shook his head. "I suppose you're right Sheriff. Thanks for your help."

"Anytime. Maybe consider getting a security camera so you know where she gets off to?"

Karl nodded, but I knew when I was being blown off. "Yeah, sure Sheriff. I'll look into it, and don't you worry, you've got my vote next election."

I guess that was that, then. "All right Karl, you and Marguerite have a good one."

I left Karl and Marguerite behind, and got on with the rest of the day, which meant doing a slow drive through town so I always knew what was going on. It didn't matter if it was domestic problems, hunger, drinking, drugs, whatever it was, I liked to know. Knowing meant I could head off situations before they became real problems. That's how you kept a town like Tulip from becoming like so many other small towns when factories fled the country and tech took over everything that was left standing.

Up and down the streets of Tulip I drove, in a grid pattern to take note of changes to neighborhoods and put a name to any new faces I saw, which weren't that many. Most of the newcomers to Tulip lately had, oddly, been female. None of them had caused much trouble, aside for the falling in love kind.

That was a kind of trouble I didn't need. The military and law enforcement was plenty of drama, I didn't need to deal with the drama of a woman in my off hours. No thanks. I wasn't interested. Which meant the matchmakers in town were as dangerous to me as any criminal. And when I saw them lately I went in the opposite direction, thank you very much.

Nothing looked out of the ordinary, and my stomach was growling like that was its primary function, so I headed back to the office where hopefully, someone had lunch waiting for me.

"Afternoon Brenda. Any messages?"

The middle-aged assistant I inherited from the last sheriff looked up at me through emerald green bifocals and a toothy grin. "None I couldn't handle. You do have a visitor though. In your office," she pointed with a mischievous smile that didn't sit well with me.

"Think you can rustle up some lunch for me?" I hated asking, but dammit this job required so much paperwork and so many meetings that I didn't have enough storage space to remember small things like eating and sleeping.

"Sure thing, Sheriff. The usual?"

I gave a short nod. "Onion rings and fries, thanks. And here some cash. Thanks Brenda."

"My pleasure. Enjoy your...meeting." I was already halfway down the hall when the oddness in her tone struck me again, and I made it two steps into my office when I figured it out.

"Ms. Scanlan, what can I do for you?" Ginger Scanlan was one of the female newcomers to Tulip. Though unlike the rest, she hadn't yet succumbed to love.

At the sound of my voice, she straightened her posture and flashed a professional smile. "Sheriff. How goes the world of crime fighting?" Her smile warmed from professional to welcoming, almost friendly even.

I wasn't buying it, just like I wasn't buying the innocent look winking back at me from hazel eyes that swirled with a rainbow of colors, gold and green and amber, just like a marble.

"Just peachy. Did you come here to report a crime?" She wouldn't be the first badge bunny to show up and try to flirt her way into an invitation to my bedroom. I didn't do groupies, period.

"Not exactly. I'm here to report *on crime*," she said with emphasis as if it was needed. "I'd like to add a police blotter to the Gazette website and that will require your cooperation."

A police blotter? "No."

She straightened her spine at that one word, as if summoning her strength. "You haven't even heard me out!"

"Don't need to. The last thing we need is you and a bunch of civilians thinking you can do my job." The last time a reporter had been allowed in my business, he'd ended up dead. No coming back from that, no matter how good your intentions or how interesting the story.

She sighed and rolled her eyes. "I don't want to do your job, Sheriff. I want there to be a record of what's happening in town, which is my right by law."

"Everybody's a lawyer all of a sudden." I walked around the desk and dropped down into the old seat that still molded to the last sheriff's ass. "Not. Interested." I hoped that was clear enough for her, because there was no way in hell I was letting her talk me into any damn thing.

Ginger stood slowly, her gaze darkening with her mood as it bore a hole right through my forehead. "I said I require your cooperation, Sheriff not your permission. I'll get what I need. One way or another."

Touché. At least she had a backbone. That was something. Something kind of sexy. "Good. Then you don't need me at all for this."

"Nope, I don't. Though I'm sure I could get some good traffic on a story about the Sheriff hiding crime statistics from the public." Without another word and that ridiculous threat lingering between us, she walked out with a sexy little swing to her hips.

"Damn reporters." I didn't know much about Ginger yet, but I would. She was a reporter which meant I automatically didn't trust her. But the fact that she'd been in town for months and no one knew much about her, was alarming. To say the least.

"Knock, knock." Brenda pushed the door open cautiously, a wary expression on her face. "Still hungry?"

"That was quick." Even on a slow day, it took Big Mama at least twenty minutes to get takeout orders ready.

"Your visitor had meant to use this as a bribe. Instead she said she'd rather you stick it where the sun don't shine." Brenda's pink cheeks only added to the humor of the moment and I couldn't help it, I laughed.

Ginger had a sense of humor, I'd give her that. And she didn't take any crap. If she wasn't looking to join in on the matchmaking fun, we might be friends. As soon as I figured out what she was up to with this sudden interest in my line of work. "If you don't plan to do as she says, I can promise it'll go somewhere the sun definitely doesn't shine."

"Oh, Sheriff," she admonished and handed the bag over along with a big stack of napkins.

"Thanks Brenda. You're the best," I told her around a

bite of burger with extra raw onions, because Ginger was a smart ass.

"Don't you forget it." She pointed one long red tipped finger in my direction and slowly backed out of the office, leaving me eat in peace.

Finally.

GINGER

*S*tupid damn Sheriff, with his handsome smirking face and gruff demeanor. What does he have to be so gruff about anyway? Serving as a small-town Sheriff had to be the easiest job in the world. Other than a few domestic squabbles and public drunkenness, not much happened around here other than a whole lot of meddling. It was a big part of the reason I accepted the job in Tulip. Safety plus salary, equals a good life in my book.

I sat in a booth inside Reese's BBQ, stewing as I watched the lunchtime crowd come and go in varying stages of exhaustion. Some still had a pep in their step, possibly about an upcoming date or a new promotion, but most looked like they were going through the motions. Even in this charming small town. Although the lunch crowd was an excellent time for people watching, which helped me come up with more ideas to keep the Gazette in a steady flow of new online traffic, there was another reason I came here for lunch.

The "Meddling Matchmakers". It was an unofficial name, given to them thanks to their love of matchmaking the Hometown Heroes, and I planned to take full advantage of their expertise. And by *full advantage*, I meant setting myself up at a table close enough to hear their conversation. I needed to find out what else I could use to keep my job and keep Mom where she belonged. I wasn't brave—or stupid—enough to put myself in their crosshairs, but I had no problem eavesdropping.

It was my right as a professional journalist.

"Want me to take your order, or should I just hook up a microphone to the old ladies' table?"

The woman, the chef and the owner stood in front of me with her long blond hair pulled into a ponytail that stuck out the back of her red and white baseball cap with the Reese's logo splashed across the front. Her light brown eyes sparkled with amusement.

I sighed, happy for the interruption. "I'll have the short rib special with the Jack D sauce. And if that mic thing is real, hook me up. Thanks." I motioned for her to sit since it looked like the lunch crowd had finally started to thin out.

Reese sat and waved the ticket in the air until a passing waiter took it from her. "Thanks."

"Hard work having the best barbecue in town?" She arched a blond brow at me and I grinned. "Best in Texas?"

"Better," she said with a small, placated smile. "And yeah, it's super hard work. But that's the price of greatness. What's new with you?"

No one in Tulip knew about my mom, not yet. I didn't

want pity, and this town had a bad case of offering up help whether you wanted it or not. But since I couldn't go to Mom for advice, I could use a sounding board other than Big Mama, who would probably attempt to threaten Tim into submission.

"Nothing much, just a run-in with the Sheriff who refused me a basic request. Which by the way, he has no authority to refuse." I'd been warned about small towns and how they could sometimes be unwelcoming to newcomers, but Tulip wasn't like that. No one in Tulip was, except the Sheriff.

"That doesn't sound like Tyson. He can be gruff, and his personal skills could use updating, but he's a good guy."

I didn't doubt that, but it really wasn't the point. "Yeah well, if he was such a good guy he wouldn't refuse this request, not when my job is on the line. And did I mention he has no *legal right* to refuse me?" I knew my voice was getting shrill, but dammit, I was frustrated. Things had been locking into place so perfectly with Rafe and Big Mama already agreeing to help. Even Hope had promised to do an article on choosing the right lingerie for your body type. Things had been going well.

So well.

Reese let out a shocked whistle. "Your job? That sucks. I wish you luck."

"Yeah, thanks." Luck had nothing to do with it, and I was mad not deterred from my goal. "Anyway, it doesn't matter, I'm just fuming while I plan."

"Tyson isn't being an asshole for no good reason,

Ginger. He has his reasons for wanting to stay out of the spotlight." She had no idea that was exactly the wrong thing to say to a journalist, but I filed that bit of information away for later. "Just go easy on him."

"I don't plan on doing anything to him. But I'm not losing my job Reese, I can't."

"Why not? Jobs are easy to come by in your field, aren't they? You could start a blog like everyone else."

I snorted a laugh. "Blog earnings won't pay the kind of money I need. Besides, blogs take a while to build up a following before they become profitable."

She frowned and leaned forward with a gleam in her brown eyes. "Gambling addict? Oh, please dear lord tell me you've got something interesting like that going on in your life?" Reese blew out a long breath and leaned back against the booth seat. "I need some excitement."

I laughed. "If a mom with early onset Alzheimer's is exciting, then yeah, I've got loads of it." In those early years it had been exciting, but not the good kind of exciting, more like terrifying. "Nothing gets your blood pumping like a burnt to hell grilled cheese at three in the morning."

"Damn, that's rough. I'm sorry to hear that."

"Me too, but the point is I'm not letting the paper close. I won't. I can't."

Reese nodded and stood. "I understand, just try not to burn any bridges while saving yourself."

"I wouldn't do that." I'd fight only as dirty as I needed to for him to give me what I wanted.

"Good. I'll send you some hushpuppies on the house."

She winked and walked away, her chef whites swallowing up her petite frame.

I had just finished typing some notes and a reminder to do some digging into Sheriff Henderson when the matchmakers showed up. Eddy, Elizabeth Vargas, Betty Kemp and Helen Landon walked in and took their designated booth, the round one in the center of the small restaurant. The women were close friends, laughing and giving each other a hard time while they decided what to order.

"Eddy, I have to say you were masterful with Scott and Stevie. By the time they realized what was going on, they were halfway in love." The awe in Betty's voice didn't escape my notice, and I barely resisted the urge to turn to see her expression.

"Thanks. He was ready for it, he just needed a good hard push. And the right woman."

"Ain't that the truth," Helen agreed. "They think they know what they want, but Scott never would've ended up with a girl like Stevie on his own." I could just imagine them all shaking their heads at the silly kids.

"A pitcher of strawberry margaritas, please!" Elizabeth's voice rang out, followed by the table erupting in laughter. "To celebrate our latest success, and to inspire us for the next one."

I shook my head at the older women who were each a force to be reckoned with on their own, together they were as unstoppable as the Avengers. The women were over the top ridiculous in their efforts, and the worst part was, they were unashamed of it, which made reporting on their antics as well as the Hometown Heroes, had stirred up a lot of traffic for the Gazette.

But it wouldn't last forever. Nothing ever did.

That thought, as depressing as it was, gave me an excellent idea. I didn't' need it to last forever, I just needed to keep traffic growing steadily for long enough to appease Tim. The calendar and fundraising were almost complete, and I'd have to come up with something else.

In the meantime, I had the Hometown Heroes.

Find out happens next with Ginger & Tyson in Cold Hearted Love!

Small Town Protectors (Tulip Series)

That Hot Night

I've known Janey my whole life, the bossy girl next door.

Always with her face hidden behind a camera.

Until one hot night, when I finally saw her. In a red dress.

She hypnotized me. Mesmerized me.

Opened my eyes to Janey, the woman.

And now that I've had a taste of her, nothing will ever be the same.

Not me.

And certainly not us.

Loving My Enemy, Book 3: An Enemies to Lovers Romance

Bad Boy Benefits, Book 2: A Roommate Hero Romance

Hero In My Bed, Book 1: A Roommate Hero Romance

Accidental Hookups

Accidentally Hitched: An Accidental Marriage Romance
(Accidental Hookups Book 1)

Accidentally Wed: An Accidental Marriage Romance (Accidental
Hookups Book 2)

Accidentally Bound: An Accidental Marriage Romance
(Accidental Hookups Book 3)

Accidentally Wifed: An Accidental Marriage Romance
(Accidental Hookups Book 4)

Boardroom Games

His Takeover: An Enemies to Lovers Romance (Boardroom
Games Book 1)

Sinful Takeover: An Enemies to Lovers Romance (Boardroom
Games Book 2)

Naughty Takeover: An Enemies to Lovers Romance (Boardroom
Games 3)

Standalones

Stranded: A Mountain Man Romance

Dating the Doctor: A Single Dad Romance

Dr. Daddy Next Door: A Single Dad Romance

Cowboy's Fake Fiancée: A Single Dad & A Virgin Romance

Cowboy's Barmaid: A Small Town Military Romance

Let's Pretend : A Fake Fiancée Romance

I'll Pretend : A Fake Fiancée Romance

Boxsets & Collections

Misters of Pleasure: A Small Town Protectors Boxset

Daddies & Nannies: A Contemporary Romance Boxset

Cowboys & Bosses: A Contemporary Romance Boxset

Kiss Me, Love Me: An Alpha Male Romance Boxset

Accidentally On Purpose:An Accidental Marriage Boxset

Small Town Misters: A Small Town Protectors Boxset

ABOUT THE AUTHOR

Piper Sullivan is an old school romantic who enjoys reading romantic stories as much as she enjoys writing them.

She spends her time day-dreaming of dashing heroes and the feisty women they love.

Visit Piper's website www.pipersullivan.com

Join Piper's Newsletter for quirky commentary, new romance releases, freebies and contests.

Check her out on BookBub

Stalk her on Facebook

Printed in Great Britain
by Amazon